Tales of a Traveling Teacher

Walking with Snow Leopards in Paradise

Book 1

Joshua Smalley

~~~

ISBN ~ 979-8-9920390-1-6

4

Table of Contents

DEDICATION 7

INTRODUCTION: THE GRAY GHOST 9

CHAPTER 1: ARRIVAL IN PARADISE 12

CHAPTER 2: STRUGGLE & SEARCH.....................................51

CHAPTER 3: SNOW LEOPARD WALK 105

THEMES 127

MESSAGE TO READER: JOIN THE JOURNEY..................133

BOOK SERIES INTRODUCTION 135

REFERENCES...139

 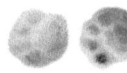

Dedication

This book is dedicated to my children: Temesgen, Rebecca, and Maleda. May you ever adventure, wander, and wonder like your father, and in doing so, each of you take a unique journey.

~~~

Also, this book is dedicated to the two guides who led me on this adventure. Without them, this book would have been impossible. Without them, my life would be missing an important and enriching experience that I will never forget.

~~~

Additionally, this book is dedicated to my travel partner. With your companionship and support, I had someone with whom I could share the journey.

Introduction:

The Gray Ghost

Snow leopards dare to be angels. Commonly referred to as the gray ghosts of the Himalayas, these near-spiritual beings defy gravity, exploring heights up to five thousand meters and temperatures as low as negative forty centigrade. These majestic beasts kiss the wingtips of the heavens and bring magic down with them to earth. They serve as liaisons between the natural and the supernatural.

When they descend into a valley, it might as well be a celestial being descending from the clouds, haloed and highlighted by heavenly lights. The snow leopard's myths and grandeur endure generation after generation, capturing the imagination of people and entire cultures. Whispers of leopards walking through villages percolate across Central and East Asia.

The hearts of us humans skip a beat, and our hair stands on end when we see the snow leopard's shape in the blustery snow. Similar to the wolf, few animals enrapture the psyche of human beings like the magnificent snow leopard.

Snow leopards live a brutal balancing act in the mountains, maneuvering on the line between extinction and survival. Human encroachment, climate change, and the natural terrain create near-impossible obstacles for survival.

Despite these challenges, the elusive and majestic white coat with black marks moves across precarious metaphorical and literal peaks, fighting for existence. Blue sheep and ibex know this precarious edge of survival all too clearly as the deft leopard dives vertically toward them, motivated by hunger. Against all odds, the gray ghost persists and thrives.

So many organizations and volunteers all around the world dedicate their work to the permanence and protection of the snow leopard. Their efforts must be praised as some of the most successful conservation and community partnership programs on the planet. Indeed, the snow leopard has either retained population numbers or increased in some

 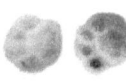

regions over recent decades. This is all due to phenomenal efforts and partnerships.

The work to protect the snow leopard should be the model adopted and modified for many conservation projects across the world. Both man and nature can thrive side by side.

Only in recent decades have people spotted the snow leopard more regularly. Up until current times, snow leopard sightings were exceedingly rare, reserved only for those brave and beautiful people who live high in the Himalayan villages. From these efforts to protect and study the animal, sightings have increased.

It is from its elusive nature, blending in perfectly with its natural camouflage, that the snow leopard earns its name: gray ghost. Furthermore, it earns its mystic status as an apex predator perched at the pinnacle of the planet's mountainous tips, rearing each new generation of vulnerable cubs in this white-washed, frozen landscape.

Therefore, to walk with snow leopards is to partake in something dreamlike. To live on the mountain's edge with them is to see life from an entirely fresh angle. It is a practice in appreciation of its greatness, power, elegance, and context.

The opportunity to see a snow leopard in its natural habitat is the highest bucket list task for many nature enthusiasts. Such an experience pushes the human body to its capacity and challenges the mind to endure such environments. To walk with the gray ghost is to play with the supernatural and feign immortality, even if for a short time.

This adventure of searching for and studying the snow leopard had called to me for decades before I finally booked a trip to India. For as long as I can remember, the snow leopard has been my favorite mammal. I have daydreamed, sketched, painted, and discussed this cat for many years. Finally, it was time for me to embark on a journey to see the gray ghost.

My adventure would come with its obstacles and its moments of elation. From first-stage frostbite to navigating near-death cliff edges for days, from enduring numb and aching limbs to surviving haunting visitations from evil in the night, from breathless treks to days of disappointment, these would form the consequences of daring to dance with the ghost of the Himalayas.

This is my story of searching for the near-invisible gray ghost.

11

Chapter 1:

Arrival in Paradise

Our Boeing 737 MAX banks hard left, pointing nose down toward a winter wonderland below. The red-tipped wings of our Spice Jet contrast starkly against a white valley backdrop that expands before us. A layered mosaic of pinpoint peaks, buried in snow, trails off almost infinitely into the horizon. Even from our elevation, the Himalayan range stretches beyond the eye's perception.

Everything here reminds me of home. I grew up near the North Cascades, where specific places such as Gothic Basin, Three Fingers, Dragontail Peak, and Mount Shuksan captured my heart and imagination as a child.

As I gaze out my window at seat F19, I reminisce on a familiar memory of crisp, silent air on sun and snow-soaked Saturday mornings at one thousand, five hundred and twenty-four meters. On rare occasions, the air would turn violent and scream wind and snow into my face. I fell in love with each experience all the same.

These mental pictures constitute my memories of home, my sanctuary: the vast wilderness and mountain ranges of my childhood. Today, I take the plunge into a new version of this same old adventure, a kind of hyper-version of home in the form of the Himalayas.

My smudged window partially obstructs the impressive view. Despite this, shapes and shadows shine through the distortions. I see a mosaic perspective of everything below. In a way, this partial view of reality sparkles with immense beauty.

Reality rests in the land below, ever so close; I can almost touch it now. I rub the glass with my sweater to wipe away the grime, but the view remains blurred. All I achieve is adding my own oily sleeve's streak to the glass. '*It's fitting, really,*' I muttered to myself silently. '*Approaching heaven*

shouldn't be in hi-definition; it's too glorious to dare absorb a precise view. It's too powerful for unfiltered access.'

I imagine I can hear the pilot announce over the hum of the engines, "Welcome to paradise, everyone. Take a look outside and soak up the view." Instead, the pilot leaves us passengers alone to absorb the vast views below, the hum from the plane's engines purring in the background. As we circle, the land stretches out even further, cold and barren, with unforgiving terrain marked by jagged, knife-like peaks.

This is what I picture heaven to be: a vast physical mural where you have only time, space, and yourself to make an adventure out of it all, to create something special out of nothing. It is a call to the unseen, untouched, and unknown. It pulls you from the mundane and into the extraordinary and risky.

I feel magnetized to the contours, peaks, gullies, and possibilities of adventure, of a blank slate of opportunity. In this particular moment, I want to teleport below into the haunting Himalayan Mountain range and examine every corner and crevice. I want to discover what lurks there in its silky-white shadows.

A world like this tests your mettle, your determination to run toward everything your biology avoids. Your biological imperative longs for comfort and safety. This land offers the opposite, along with the rewards only found if the call to adventure is answered.

My eyes continue darting around, even with an obstructed view, dancing along each new pristine peak while my mind wanders. *'In fact, I think hell would be a temperature-controlled room, forced to lounge in an extra soft couch. You must wear a fluffy, warm robe and puffy slippers. You are obliged to constant massages every thirty minutes. You are compelled to watch sitcoms and eat your favorite guilty pleasure snacks throughout the day.*

There's one caveat: there is no escape from any of these conditions for eternity. This, for me, would be pure hell. No adventure? No conflict to overcome? No opportunity to grow? Only comfort? I can feel the cozy claustrophobia closing in on me already.'

We continue banking left, making full circles down into the valley below and toward the airport. I start to make out the landing strip in the

 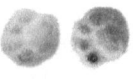   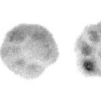

distance amongst the smattering of homes. The stewardesses take their final seats and fasten their seat belts; a subtle look of calm rests on their eyelids.

As the plane turns, sunlight dances in through the windows, whirling in motion around the inside cabin. The spectacle alights our morning landing with a kaleidoscope of glistening shards of light. '*The perfect welcome.*'

Whenever I travel in airplanes, an overwhelming feeling of "there" consumes me. Peering out my oval window, I notice many "there" places throughout the flight. I feel a longing to live in each "there," and yet each one remains agonizingly out of my reach, floating past me below.

For example, I might spot a small village somewhere in Central Asia and dream of a different life where it was my birthplace and culture. Or I fly over a city in Kenya and wonder how different life would be "there." I travel over middle America and consider managing a fifty-acre farm. Or I soar over a small village in Europe and imagine life's pace in these quaint towns.

Sometimes I want very specific "there" experiences. I want to taste homemade stew in Borneo, forage for food in the rainforests of Nicaragua, own a steaming banya and Siberian log cabin deep in the heart of Russia, or craft Newari woodcarvings in a forgotten Nepali village.

Sometimes, the desire hits closer to home in a small town with its one café and its worn-out, dusty billiards table under dimly lit bulbs. In this room, stories linger until morning through musky cigarette clouds. Each "there," whether specific or general, begs me to dwell, experience, see, and understand.

Then again, maybe my desires are naïve, even greedy, or foolishly romantic. The places I see with rose-colored glasses may, in reality, be fraught with pain and problems. Possibly, the real gleaning is that all humans and their cultures are cut from the same rock. Every "there" might be the same as the next.

Yet, my longing persists. It tugs at me deeply, constantly. I refuse to die ignorant of most human experiences. The world's playground must be played. This has become my obsessive quest. I want to know the drama, danger, and delight of each little "there" I can experience.

Sudden turbulence rattles me out of my mindful wandering. We drop probably ten meters instantly. With this drop, my stomach leaps upward inside my body. Personal items around the cabin fly, sprawling all around us. A few overhead bins jar loose, suitcases threatening to fall on heads.

I clench the armrests in a rush of panic, as my seat shakes violently. Adrenaline pulsates throughout my body, and it takes a minute or two for my heart and the plane's rocking to subside. *'Descending at this elevation, in these temperatures, must make turbulence particularly bad.'* Once the plane returns to a smooth glide, we make what seems like our final curve before touching down.

I see spiderwebbed trails of roads and small buildings come into view. The emerald Zanskar River winds alongside each of these roads, weaving its way through the valley; I studied the region before coming, and mere facts found in text now materialize in front of me. Everything I see calms the angst from the flight.

As we drop lower into the valley, I see small white caps moving along the river, chunks of ice in a contorting cocktail of bobbing chaos, flowing in rapid currents. Every few seconds, ice plates crashing against each other catch a sparkle of sunlight and beam it back to my viewpoint inside the plane. The river's brilliance winks its deadly chill at us.

I am not alone. Traveling with me is my companion, Radmir. The flight is sparse, so we both chose window seats in back-to-back rows. I can see him just over the headrest. He is tall, a good ten centimeters taller than I. He's slender, but well-built, wiry, and ready for the challenge of scaling frozen mountains every waking hour for fourteen straight days.

Radmir has dark, wavy hair and the beginnings of a beard. He wears black boots with gray laces and green, multi-toned camo pants. A thick, brown jacket covers his upper body, and his black liner gloves poke out from his left pocket.

As he peers out his window, I can see the slight tremble in his hands. *'Is it from excitement? Sure. Worry? Absolutely. Hope? Yes, that too.'* The concern

of not seeing anything at all after two weeks in this winter wilderness occupies our thoughts. We are about to embark on a physically strenuous and bone-chilling journey; we want a reward for our toils.

We met at a quaint bar in Uzbekistan. I was on vacation, visiting Samarkand and all its magnificence, while he traveled there, along with his wife, for a work conference. His wife, Nazgul, accompanied us that night. Right away, we all found common interest in topics of nature and wildlife.

Radmir works as a civil engineer; trekking is a nice diversion from his office space life. Once the discussion of snow leopards emerged, we knew this trip would be our common destiny. From that day forward, we kept in contact and began planning a once-in-a-lifetime trip.

I glance back at him in the row behind me. He flashes his teeth in a wide smile and heaves a hearty laugh; we are finally here. Radmir's bursting laugh and deep voice are the perfect yin-yang for the trip.

For me, his voice symbolizes the depth of what we hope will be our experience. Mixed with his laugh, his voice symbolizes the pure stupidity of it all. Two silly people journeying into the white-washed Himalayas, oppressed by torturous temperatures, in search of a ghost, the snow leopard. Beautiful madness. Purely preposterous and naively impossible. Heaven.

His wife was with us at the beginning of our trip to India, but she had plans with friends in New Delhi. The night before we flew to Ladakh, we enjoyed a meal of Chicken Tikka Masala and Masala Chai, and then he said goodbye to Nazgul.

Both excitement and fear loom in our minds. I let my imagination take control: '*Soon enough, we will be on a cliff's edge, in utter silence, boots nudging pebbles off the sheer ledge. We will be ghosts, mere whispers in the wind on these sheer ledges, almost invisible in the ebb and flow of clouds and lost in a colossal sea of peaks and snow.*'

I look at Radmir and see, not only the tremble in his hands, but now a tinge of apprehension in his eyes as they dart back and forth, surveying the landscape from his window. He lets out another laugh, this time more nervous-sounding than before. At this point, I feel the same worry, but it manifests as a rapidly tapping leg.

We hold no fear of death, only the fear of failing to lay eyes upon the evasive snow leopard. Lost in the blistery blizzards on serrated edges, seeing the perfectly camouflaged snow leopard feels nearly impossible.

Our guides on the ground will bring their expertise, but nature has its own mind; you may see ten ghosts, you may see none. Truth be told, we are about to embark on a journey where the destination, or desired result, may never be achieved.

Despite this, we remain hopeful with steadied anticipation; we have a good idea of what we will face mentally and physically up there in that vertical wilderness.

Radmir slaps his brown beanie on his head in preparation for landing, takes a deep breath, swallowing down anxiety. Doing this leaves more room for excitement. I feel I should do the same, but my mouth is too dry to conjure it.

The tarmac nears; only about one hundred meters before we touch down. Rows of ridges now form a stark, pointed pattern in the direction of the city, ebbing down from their illustrious heights in the heart of the Himalayan range into the gulley below.

My eyes follow the ridge's path until it merges with roads, and then small shacks, and lastly larger homes and a few hotels. This is where civilization kisses the feet of these marvelous mountains. The entire landscape points down into this city as if to say, "This is where you belong, right here. Right 'there.'"

In this instant, it is a rare moment where a "there" possibility converges with my lived reality; I may now dwell with the beautiful, brilliant, and bold people of Leh, the capital of Ladakh, along with their illustrious resident, the snow leopard.

Polar air punches me in the face as I disembark the plane and shuffle onto the jet bridge. This is Leh's greeting in December. Leh offers a

 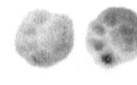

hearty 'how do you do', clocking in at approximately negative twenty-five degrees Celsius.

Mountains are my forte; I come prepared. Before landing at Kushok Bakula Rimpochee Airport, I added several layers of outdoor attire: a blue goose down summit jacket, a black thermal bottom and top, a purple beanie, and two pairs of gray liner gloves.

With each step off the plane and into these unforgiving temperatures, my trekking boots grip and stick to the tooth-textured, gray bridge. In times of ever-present ice, sky bridges like these prove useful. If only we could borrow these to traverse the slick mountains for the next two weeks.

We scamper across the snow and ice-topped tarmac and into the airport, which, in reality, is a small baggage claim tent and an accompanying building with a few white, plastic seats for departures. Freezing air continues to grip us as the building is partially open to the elements; every word from the airport staff curls into puffs of mist in front of their lips.

It is so cold, I can barely hear them speak, as my ears ring numb. I feel my fingertips ache at the tips already, and this is with gloves. Moments like this may prompt a person to question their life decisions. *'Am I sane? Why didn't I choose the pristine Bentota Beach in southern Sri Lanka or an eco-friendly bungalow in Aruba?'* Anyone with a weak constitution might dash back to the warmth of the plane, begging for a reunion with New Delhi.

Not me. I shutter these adventure-pillaging thoughts away from consciousness and bask in the frigid wonderland surrounding me and the airport. I am here, in paradise. *'Breathe.'*

I remind myself that I desire adventure that pushes the limits, finding myself muttering another self-speech to get me into the right mindset. The severity of the biting temperatures threw me off, and now I need a mental reset. *'Lofty ambitions like chasing snow leopards in the Himalayas demand sacrifice and endurance. Otherwise, everyone would pursue this experience. No one would be filtered out.'*

As my mind continues this monologue, I look over at Radmir. He seems to be locked into the same headspace. Under our breath, we mumble to ourselves. The game is real now. I return to my inner thoughts. '*Life is too short to dabble solely in the mundane. An occasional spark of the impossible makes life bearable.*' Simple, yet effective, platitudes such as these keep me focused.

No inclement weather forecasts or sheer ice cliffs will stand in my way. So, '*Bring on the punches, Leh; I was made for these moments.*' I chuckle to myself at my naïve bravado. Little do I know what stands before me on this trip.

We collect our checked-in luggage at the single-belt baggage claim zone. Even now, the body grows stiff, and movements at this elevation and temperature remind me that this is no longer New Delhi, where we had resided the past two nights. We have swapped humid heat with numbing temperatures.

My North Face bag hangs heavily in my hand, bulging with gear. With everything from layers of trekking clothes to water containers to camera gear, I feel prepared but burdened by it all. I need just a couple of minutes for a quick confirmation that everything is still in place. To ensure nothing has been left behind, I unzip each compartment and look. After this, we move toward the passport control queue.

We pass through swiftly; no one wants to remain in the elements too long. '*This should be the setup at every passport control station; make the room so frigid that the line moves rapidly.*' As we walk out of the small airport building and into the parking lot, we meet our guides.

As we approach them on the other side of the parking lot, my nose hairs freeze stiff, and a salty tear, forming in the corner of my left eye from the chilled wind, sticks to the side of my face. '*Even salty things freeze here?*' Everything is perfect. Pure paradise.

I suck in the stinging air, allowing the pain to inform my lungs of what to expect these next fourteen days. Somehow, it feels colder than when we first exited the plane. I grip my luggage with resolute resolve against the tyranny of the wintry reality and move forward.

 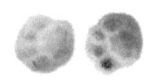

The first guide to greet us is Padma. She is a beautiful young Ladakhi. She is short, but she carries a confidence that far exceeds her physical height. She has black trekking pants, a thick gray sweater, a camouflage beanie hat, and a warm smile. Wavy, black hair curls out from the back of her hat and rests on her shoulders. Everything she wears is pristine and well-kept. As she approaches us, Padma boasts an intentional and methodical gait.

Padma leans forward toward us and offers a firm handshake and a hearty "Jullay," or hello. Her hands have known difficult times, given the rough lines and calluses; overall, her physical strength impresses me.

Her face holds youthfulness, lacking the wrinkles that come with years of harsh winters and wisdom. Instead of creases written across her face, she holds wisdom in her eyes. I can see generations of insight passed down to her, floating in her pupils. They shift between dilation and constriction, back and forth. I find her eyes hypnotic.

Padma then turns and greets Radmir as Dorje, our second guide, steps forward. He approaches us in a humbler disposition. He slightly bows and extends his hand to us, shuffling in small steps.

He wears a checkered, yellow and blue flannel top with lime green Columbia trekking pants. I see the familiar diamond-shaped insignia and bold lettering on the right chest pocket. His black boots shine brightly from meticulous care, just like Padma. His boots reflect a bit of the sun as it continues to poke through the clouds above.

He holds a gentle posture that hints at a deep sense of knowing. Both Padma and Dorje seem to hold a wealth of knowledge in their mere presence. I can already perceive that he understands the journey ahead and keeps his optimism in check. We are yet another tourist team, beaming with foolish glee under fresh legs. He knows how to handle us.

Despite his awareness of our ignorance, he offers a welcoming aura, an openness, a willingness to try new things. It is in his smile, his handshake grip, and his posture. He radiates a desire to put faith in these new visitors to Leh. His steadying presence helps regulate my own heart and breathing rhythms.

I had failed to notice my breath remaining shallow for some time. My heart rate had been elevated. '*Maybe it is the elevation. It could be the inner stir of mixed emotions. It could also be the mere presence of these two people in front of me, Padma and Dorje.*' With a calming heart and a couple of sharp, deep breaths, I re-center my wandering thoughts back on Dorje and Padma.

I feel a new wave of energy. '*This must be the adrenaline rush adventure seekers such as whitewater kayakers refer to just before jumping headfirst into a raging river. All this and we are still in the airport parking lot.*' I cannot help but see myself as a child in a candy shop.

Dorje seems pleased with our appearance of physical fitness. "You both seem young and strong. We will walk the mountains. We will all climb very far every day."

I smile and flex my jaw in determination to live up to these first impressions. '*Bring on the Himalayas.*'

"We will do whatever it takes to find the snow leopard. We are ready," I assure our guides with a confident smile. Radmir nods in agreement.

"Have you hike a mountain before?" asks Padma. She seems more skeptical of first impressions and seeks more reassurance of our abilities.

"We've both trekked mountains in several countries. I hope we're up for the challenge." I speak a bit too fast, but they get the gist of what I am saying.

After we exchange a few more pleasantries, complete our initial introductions, and hoist all the gear into the back of their van, it is time to depart. We hop in through the side door and head to our hotel for a day of acclimatization in Leh.

I figure this ride is the perfect time to play some rock music from the back seat and get our minds into the right headspace. We are about to face Mother Nature in all her power and beauty.

If lucky, we might even see the crown jewel of her showcase—the snow leopard. The battle before us necessitates a kind of mental grit, one mixed with awe, respect, strength, understanding, risk-taking, and patience.

My band of choice: ACDC. My song of choice: "Thunderstruck." The music blasts from our speaker in the back seat. Our guides seem immediately pleased with the choice; their slight in-rhythm nods align with the pulsating beats as we maneuver the winding, narrow streets of Leh. Already, I can see playfulness in both Padma and Dorje. *How can't you be playful? Your work is to explore God's masterclass of nature craftsmanship; their office is other-worldly.*

High rock walls on either side of the road obstruct our view of the homes and yards. Even still, I see the tips of what appear to be beautiful homes splashed against the vast mountainous backdrop.

Around each tight bend, our driver honks, warning oncoming cars of our presence. Navigating these corners can be a game of chicken. *'Who will give in first? Who has the legal right of way?'* I wonder. *'Life on the edge, even down here in the valley. Pure Heaven.'*

The vivacious blast of arpeggios brings me back to our 'mindset prep.' Radmir plays air guitar, headbanging for added effect, and I join. He swirls his hair in mesmerizing circles with each head bang. My hair is short, but I match his intensity. Soon enough, a tinge of vertigo grips me, and I am forced to pause.

Our excitement and fear finally have a physical outlet valve after hours of quiet, confined, and subdued travel in taxis and planes. The nervous energy emanates from us and rattles the van.

While we behave like toddlers rocking out in the back, the mature, doubting side plagues our minds with lingering thoughts: *'How ignorant to expect to see an animal with adjectives such as "elusive" or "ghost"? All this effort, preparation, and cost will likely end in futility?'*

Peter Matthiessen once discovered this harsh reality and felt privileged to trek for two months, searching for the snow leopard. He found solace and beauty in the journey and the people, resolving to accept the invisible nature of the gray ghost.

That the leopard avoided him cemented its mystique; it was almost better for him to have never seen the snow leopard. Call me greedy, but I want the journey and the reward. I will appreciate the beastly voyage, and I will find the beauty as well.

When we arrive at the hotel, Padma and Dorje step out, stretch, and bid us adieu as they head out to do some last-minute prep work. They show a steadfast confidence in their smiles and physical presence, shoulders erect and pulled back. They tell us they will stay in a different home during the evening after they finish their trip into town.

"Goodbye. Tomorrow, we go," says Dorje as he hitches his backpack to one shoulder.

"It is a pleasure meeting you both," Radmir says, looking for any indication that they think we are viable trekkers capable of this journey.

"Yes. Thank you," responds Padma, a slight smile forming. Both she and Dorje wear dark sunglasses that hide their eyes. For Radmir and me, it is difficult to ascertain what they think of us without the glasses, let alone with them. '*Well, maybe that's better if we don't know what they think. I suppose I don't want to know at this point.*'

We will mostly rest during our first night in Leh. Acclimatization is our primary goal. After checking in, we settle into our separate rooms and rest in our warm beds for a couple of hours. The thrust of icy air has shocked us into a sleepy stupor. The sudden elevation gain played a role, too.

The room's accommodations are simple: a bed, a television, a couple of tables, and a bathroom. The interior walls are stripped down to their bare, brown wood. A few cheap frames are attached to the walls near the entrance door and sit off-center. One is a reprint of a faded, snowy landscape painting. The other is the Dalai Lama. A wobbly, brown table holds some tea packets, cups, and a kettle. Otherwise, the room is bare.

Again, for me, this is paradise. I need only the basic necessities. The bed feels warm in comparison to the chill of Leh. This is all I need. Our team will spend our time in the magical outdoors, so we have little need for an amenity-heavy hotel.

After some resting time, we eventually stir and wake up just an hour past lunchtime. Feeling fresh and rejuvenated from the nap, we meet in the hallway and head downstairs for some bread, soup, and curry.

As we finish and wash up, we decide to explore the hotel area and possibly the town. "Let's layer up and walk around a bit. I've got some energy now and I want to see what this area has to offer," suggests Radmir.

"Absolutely. I've got some energy. Let's do it." Every day's task should be an adventure. *'This means one has to choose to see daily life as an adventure. This place is a natural adventure, but can I carry this same perspective home?'*

Something I notice right away around the hotel is the Endless, or Eternal, Knot symbol. I find it throughout the property, on fences, walls, and furniture. As we move beyond the property itself, I see it in several places throughout the neighborhood.

Peeling back my black Columbia sweater on my left forearm, I take a fresh glance at my Eternal Knot tattoo. This symbol has meant so much to me in life, especially in the darker times. My connection with this place heightens immediately.

I love this tattoo. The intertwined lines form a mesmerizing pattern across my entire forearm. It is a complex design with a multitude of meanings.

The meanings, symbolized in this single shape, include life's complexities, the entire cycle of life and death, human destruction and beauty, compassion, human madness and sanity, the interconnectedness of everything, wisdom, and the duality and paradoxes of existence.

For comparison, I lift my arm next to another Eternal Knot symbol on the side of a building. Identical shapes. I place my right hand on the tattoo, close my eyes, and whisper to myself, *"Life is terribly beautiful.'*

My eyes move from the building to its backdrop to gaze on the ominous mountain range directly behind. Terribly dangerous, hauntingly beautiful. *'Terribly beautiful is this trip—reaching the frosted pinnacles of the Himalayas, one step from death and one step from seeing the magnificent gray ghost.*

The entire absurdity of this trip summed up perfectly within one simple design.' I glance back at my tattoo; I am home. This is heaven. I am "there."

We move along the streets and through the neighborhood. Radmir holds a small point-and-shoot camera, capturing mostly buildings and people. He is so enraptured by the moment that he has no idea I have fallen a couple of blocks behind. Not wanting to lose him, I pick up my pace to catch up. Breathing feels labored already on this flat surface and at this humble elevation.

Another element of this place that catches my attention as we walk about is its architecture. Mixing Central Asian, Indian, and Tibetan designs, Leh boasts a uniquely beautiful and rugged look. Most houses are squared off in concrete and pristine, white, textured plaster, only to be accented by large, polished, hand-carved, brown window frames.

These juxtaposed textures create a spectacle for the eyes. The window frames are lattice-like, with hand-crafted markings in the wood. The entire vertical landscape of snow-capped peaks stands behind these stately homes of white and rich brown, framing them aesthetically.

Adding to the visual delight of the town, mounted on each home are multi-colored prayer flags, pinned to the roof or balconies. These serve as a splash of color set against the colossal, white-washed scenery.

They explode with flapping, vigorous energy as each gust comes cascading down through the valley, originating from high in the peaks above. The sound of these flags whipping in the wind contributes a pitter-patter rhythm to the otherwise quiet neighborhood.

Once again, I am made aware of the elevation. I consciously gulp air, forgetting to breathe carefully, deeply, and with regularity. Just a few breaths taken unconsciously, and I feel dizzy immediately. Every breath needs to be deliberate and deep. My awkward and rapid breath jolts me from my hypnosis of the entire neighborhood scene.

With a few more breaths, I regain my stability and resume gawking at the views. Mountains tower over the town like governing deities. *'How is this real?'*

    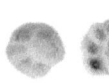

Radmir notices me whispering to myself. "I don't even know how to put words to what we are seeing right now," he says, eyes unable to be peeled from the street. "I need to pinch myself."

"I know. This view has sucked the words out of my mouth. Well, that and the elevation and cold. I'm completely bewildered by the magnificence of this place. Could you imagine living here?"

"Well, that's quite a leap; it would be hard living. The difference between the harsh reality of life here and our pampered city lives is quite stark. I'm not so sure we could do it. But I'm completely awe-struck regardless." Radmir lifts his camera to his brow again and captures a few more shots, and says, "Pictures will fail to do this place justice."

"It's amazing how we can capture this moment with a lens while knowing that the capture is inadequate. How can it be? You'd think the lens would be the most objective collector of this moment. But you're right, these photos will fall flat in comparison to reality." Slowly, one shuffled step after another, I rotate around to obtain a panoramic sense of it all.

I keep my camera mostly at my side. I need to take it all in, fully. Too often, I have the camera raised, and I miss the moment. That said, at other times, especially with wildlife, to have the lens to my eye is to be more engaged than a mere passive viewer. If I am capturing the moment, then I am considering light, wind, season, storytelling, angles, composition, camera settings, animal behavior, safety, and so much more.

For me, I liken it to the difference between being on stage acting compared to being an audience member watching the play. Both participate. However, is it fair to say the actors fail to participate in the moment? Maybe they participate at an even higher level than the audience. Might it be that someone taking a photo of a moment is a more engaged actor than those passively viewing the scene?

All this to say, bringing a camera out is not immediately a failure to be in the moment. Nonetheless, on the main street in Leh, I decide to keep the lens at my side.

Every few steps brings about more visual delights. Only an environment like Leh can act as a welcoming ground just before entering the hallowed heavens of the snow leopard. *'It's only fitting to lose my breath, literally, in this place as it welcomes me to the heavens above. I have had my breath taken away.'*

Radmir notices my odd behavior—not taking photos and constantly pausing. I usually move like a blur, all while the lens is positioned prominently in my hand. But not in this moment for some reason. Life has slowed, and I cannot help but pause and see it all.

Just the fact that Radmir notices my change is indicative of who he is. He is the kind of friend you need at your side. He watches closely and makes himself present when necessary. He walks up to me and asks, "You good?" Radmir uses a half whisper, careful not to disrupt any possible meditative state I have achieved.

"Yes, I'm good." I pause for a breath. "I just love it here already. A bit winded. Gotta get used to this elevation. Man, pacing and breathing are all a wreck right now."

"Me too." With his left hand occupied by his camera, he uses his teeth to pull his right glove off to adjust his laces on his boots. Radmir knows my pace in life; he knows that lacing up is necessary as I may suddenly launch into warp speed mode at any minute.

I love living at a pace that maximizes opportunities: up early and out often. *'Life is too short to waste it sitting around and waiting. We only have a few thousand breaths we've been gifted in life. I must spend mine exploring.'*

After he adjusts his laces, we head quickly toward the main part of town. Our time is brief; we have but one day to visit the main street. We hustle to the town's center, winding in and out of each mazed road.

Spirals of smoke collect in a near-distant point ahead, indicating a market in the distance. We aim in this direction, tiptoeing and peering over the high residential walls to catch a glimpse and maintain general direction. After a few more blocks in the icy afternoon, barely detectable murmurs of a bustling market echo in the alleys and continue to lead in the same direction as the smoke overhead.

 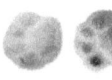   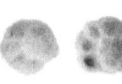

As we continue our struggle to catch our breath, we find ourselves elated by the surprise of each twist and turn of the winding roads, intriguing landscapes, and designs.

At this moment, a massive dog bursts out from a slightly opened entrance gate to a home. He explodes into the street, barking with tooth-threatening vigor. With huge tufts of hair flowing and bouncing from his movements, I think this might be the mastiffs I had read about before the trip. This is a common dog bred by the Ladakhi people.

I jump with fright at the sudden disruption to our calm stroll. My eyes lock wildly onto him, and fear grips me immediately. It is flight or fight time. He is up on me within seconds.

Radmir glances at me with wide eyes and lifts his arms, preparing for face and neck protection. In this instant, like Radmir, I crouch into a position ready to engage in self-defense.

With the hysterical dog's final lunges toward us, I can see his sharp canines and the spittle of saliva splashing about.

The dog stops just short of reaching us, barking pure evil. My legs give a bit underneath me, and I stumble backwards, while still maintaining balance. Radmir starts moving backwards as well. As we move, so does the dog, closing in slowly now.

After a few minutes, the dog's owner appears at the gate and whistles his dog back. Radmir and I are left panting with hands still outstretched in defensive positions, watching unflinchingly until the dog is safely away. The owner waves to us and then barks at the dog, shooing it demonstratively back into the home.

"That was something," admits Radmir.

My panting is so pronounced; I struggle to eke out a word. "Yeah. Something."

Finally, we regain the strength under our legs and decide to continue on our previous path. Dogs or no dogs, we want to see more. We turn a corner and arrive at the whirling bustle and color of the main street and its markets.

The entire street bursts alive before us in every corner, bubbling and thriving in full defiance of the frigid air. Like a sudden entrance into a theme park, we enter, wide-eyed. This is no theme park; this is their real life manifested like a musical before us. As with so many towns in Central Asia, the Silk Road's richness and diversity pepper across the dizzying flow of people, animals, food, and products.

Bright displays of fruits and vegetables next to a mosaic of textiles collide in an optical burst of colors. These stand in contrast to rows of stalls bulging at the seams with electronics, which then sit next to a bakery and its swirling heat waves emanating from the inside. All this stands against that majestic, snowy, vertical-peak backdrop.

Children cackle and chase each other across the cobblestone, waking thick-haired dogs from their afternoon slumber in the sun. Radmir and I hesitate and ensure the dogs return to their sleepy state before continuing on down the street. Negotiations and bartering murmur at every stand and grow to a steady crescendo as we move near. The movement of this market sways in mesmerizing waves.

The choreography ebbs and flows in a perfect, synergistic dance. Donkeys carry bags of grain, one merchant dashes across the street with small change in a raised hand, three girls in bright colored clothes stare and giggle at us, and a stack of metal poles slams to the ground with a stark "wham" after a man cuts the bundle free.

Radmir's head swivels back and forth, as does mine. *'There's too much to take in.'* We walk slowly through the street, which must stand out against the energized flow of everyone else.

I find myself dodging and weaving, like a character in a video game. A woman slides past me with several three-meter-long rebar poles. I whip to the left to miss her, only to be nearly stampeded by three young men carrying large sacks of flour. Right after spinning away from them, I knock into a wheelbarrow full of potatoes, moved swiftly by a man likely in his seventies.

Finally, I leap out of this highway and find safety near an onion vendor. The vendor smiles at me; *'He no doubt spotted us trying to escape the river of*

charming chaos and stumble out of harm's way. It must be comical seeing foreigners navigate this market.'

Radmir makes his way through it all with only a brush up against a donkey carrying a cart full of long wooden poles. Dusty gray streaks run across his pants as evidence. After we gather ourselves from our first encounters in the middle of the street, Radmir and I continue on our way through the market to see more fascinating spectacles.

Darting stares and occasional smiles show on each vendor's face as we walk past. We stand out, but we feel we belong. Several vendors offer welcoming hand gestures, encouraging us to visit their stall. Music lingers in the background, a peculiar and vaguely joyous melody of chanting choral mantras in a chord progression unfamiliar to me.

A faint aroma fills the air from a couple of food stalls. It seems like a mixture of steaming onions and succulent beef with herbs. The scent wraps its arms around Radmir and me until the Arctic air cuts through, and it fades away.

These sounds and smells build into the tapestry of the experience. Our senses grow aflame with so many inputs. *'I could spend days here, learning people's names and understanding what it feels like to be here, live here, and thrive here. I want to know the influencers, socialites, revolutionaries, gurus, and inspirational figures. I want to learn the music I heard and taste the meal we smelled. But we have a date with snow leopards up in the Rumbak valley tomorrow. This "there" will have to be short-lived.'*

I entreat my nose, eyes, and ears to absorb as much as possible. In a place this cold, with so much to see, there is only enough energy to observe for now. Over tea, in a warm spot someday later in life, Radmir and I can talk about this first day in Leh in its sensory-filled details.

My mind records everything carefully, and I keep repeating to myself under my breath: *'I must remember this day.'* Once we reach the end of the street, Radmir suggests that "We head back. By the time we find our way through the twisting roads to our place, it might be dark and definitely colder."

"That's a good point. Let's get moving." I pivot and head back toward our hotel and into the wave of chaos on the street. Some wave at us, some do not notice us at all, and others continue to stare. We make our way out of the market and back into the winding streets.

The return trip proves easy enough, and I take one last glance at the Eternal Knot shapes at the entrance of our hotel. *'May this symbol be the representation of our trip.'* I slightly bow my head for some reason, maybe out of some feeling of respect. Radmir has already entered the hotel and is sitting for some tea before dinner is served, and I join him. Breathing continues under duress.

Dinner is served hot with meat stew, vegetables, and bread. We finish and walk up the stairs to our rooms for the night. Warmed by dinner, my stomach feels satiated and comfortable; however, my limbs shudder in the chill of the hallway to my room. The room key tremors in my hand as I swiftly open the door and rush to the warmth of the bed.

The next morning, breakfast brings a touch of westernization—hot sausages, over-easy eggs, steaming porridge, buttered toast, apricot jam, local honey, and chilled milk. Simplicity. Beauty. Heaven. This meal is a necessity, a calm before our pending storm. We understand the importance of a night's sleep and a hearty breakfast before trekking.

The honey contains chunks of honeycomb, which reminds me of the honey markets I used to visit in Kazakhstan when I worked there. Before Kazakhstan, I had no idea that honey could be green, brown, black, purple, red, blue, and so many other colors, depending on the flower the bees pollinate.

Even thickness can vary greatly. A honey may be extremely thick, like molasses, or very runny and thin like watery syrup. The comb pieces heighten my connection to the natural state of things, unfiltered, unprocessed.

Radmir and I are the only ones present for breakfast. The sun peeks through the windows, highlighting the curling steam from our meal and drinks. It feels impossible, as if we are fictitious characters in a scene from a book steeped in magical realism. We eat in silence; talking will only deaden and diminish our capacity to cherish this moment.

 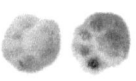

After breakfast, we pack everything into the van and begin our journey to Rumbak and into the stunning mountains overhead. The trek starts by car. We see a few urial grazing along the river. We cross via a massive steel bridge, gray and tinged blue, and then struggle up a steep incline on a rocky road. The van maintains a slow speed due to rough conditions. Each new bend reveals more rocks, peaks, and snow. Most of the region looks barren with little vegetation.

We travel about forty-five minutes up and then pull to the side of the road. The trip then evolves into a few hours of trekking on foot with the aid of our fellow companions who carry the bulk of our burdened load— donkeys. We only need to carry our daypacks.

This choice to go by foot is purposeful because it begins testing our ability to maneuver at this elevation with weight on our backs and snow under our feet. Dorje and Padma watch us closely, assessing our abilities. They walk with casual smiles. I hear them speak softly to each other. A stir of gentle laughter floats between the two of them. 'I wish I could understand their jokes and share this experience with them.'

We walk the road to the Rumbak valley. It is relatively well-kept but still rocky and uneven at times. Elevation sickness is a very real threat at this point in our journey, and so we pace ourselves.

Both Radmir and I have extensive experience at higher elevations, so we trust our bodies, and we take it slowly. 'One step, ensure a strong foothold, and now breathe. Take the next step, ensure no slippage on the rough scree. Breathe. Repeat.' It is so early in my acclimatization and trekking routine that I have to manually think through my processes until they again become automated.

I have led many treks in many countries. On rare occasions, portable oxygen has to be used to mitigate the effects of elevation sickness.

One time, the entire trip was jeopardized as a member of our team became frighteningly ill from altitude sickness. She suddenly collapsed to the ground in pain from a severe headache. She began vomiting and could not stand due to dizziness. Our team rushed her down to lower elevations and administered aid. This looming evil—elevation sickness—can strike anyone at any time.

Early on, I notice the struggle. I know my camera and its lens, along with a scope I have brought, make up most of the weight in my bag, but this is a necessary burden. Without these tools, seeing the snow leopard will be nearly impossible. Muscles quiver under the strain. I attempt to straighten my back, but it bends slightly under the weight.

Each breath knives me from within. Lungs heave and jerk from the sharpness of the cold with each intake of air. I feel like I am sipping needles through a straw. Despite all this, I know I am prepared for this trek. I clench my jaw and remain resolute with each step forward.

After about an hour of walking, I feel my second wind begin. My body welcomes the struggle, and I start to feel more alive with the feelings of my childhood in the mountains.

My calves firm up, and my knees warm under the constant pressure. I begin to feel the rhythm of my breathing settle into place. It is as if my body says, *'Thank you for returning me to my first love; I am home at these elevations.'* Every muscle fiber, every tendon, lights up and feels so good.

I glance back and see Radmir shuffling slowly. He is steady in his pace but deliberate and slow. We both labor, meditating on the purpose of this journey.

Padma and Dorje trudge on as if nothing hinders them. They continue their playful jabs at each other and remain a few meters behind us, no doubt continuing their observations. Silently, Radmir and I continue along. *'I wonder what they think of us at this point. Have we lived up to their initial impressions? Do we show any signs of weakness?'*

Most flora and fauna prove scarce in this region of the mountains. We walk among rocks, patches of ice, some dustings of snow, and soft layers of dirt.

After the second hour, Radmir seems to be in a good place physically, and I, likewise, feel strong. We find an effective pattern for breathing and establish a comfortable pace while taking in the uneven, frosty path. I close in a bit on Radmir and lean over. "Heart rate feels good, legs are good, backpack weight isn't too taxing. How's it for you?"

"Yeah, things are good," whispers Radmir behind his balaclava. At this point, we decide to walk side by side. The road is still wide enough to do this comfortably. Walking together helps us regulate our pacing and get in sync with each other. We can discover what works for both of us, and we can ensure our efforts are matched for the next two weeks. Padma and Dorje give us this freedom to trek at our own rate, and we use this to our advantage.

After a short time, they both approach us to see how we are doing. "Everything okay? Do you feel strong?" Dorje asks, almost assuming he already knows the answer. He sees us both labor and push forward; he sees us facing the difficulties of the elevation and temperatures. Despite these circumstances, he sees us push forward with strength.

"We're good," assures Radmir, slightly out of breath.

"Always keep drinking water," reminds Padma. She can tell we are experienced trekkers at this point, and she also knows that reminders are helpful. We know the critical value of hydration, especially at higher elevations.

The higher we trek, the more frigid our reality becomes. Frozen crystals form fancy patterns on each rock we pass. Closing in on us from all sides are the towering cliffs whose treacherous edges hold the secrets of snow leopard lore.

'When was the last time a snow leopard walked past this corner?' I wonder to myself. That thought immediately bounces to an entirely different idea. 'At any moment, a boulder might come cascading down off the sky-high cliff edges overhead and send us scrambling for our lives.' Normally, I traverse mountains without fear. 'The fresh terrain and new environment must be getting to me a bit.'

At the outset of this day, this is the ping-pong of my thinking, a parallel dance between thoughts of terror and thoughts of elation. I figure that an intentional leaning into positive thoughts will uplift my demeanor and strengthen my stamina for the duration of this adventure.

So, I pull myself from those thoughts and return to thinking about this hallowed ground I have entered. I begin daydreaming about a snow leopard sighting here and now. 'Surely, a snow leopard must already see us or *hear us. Certainly, she's peering down at us now, scoffing at our futile attempts to enter her domain.'* Thoughts wander further into "what ifs" and potential sightings. *'I bet Radmir is wondering the same things.'*

I imagine a sudden snow leopard head popping into our view sixty meters above. Or a leopard chuff that echoes along our path, erecting all of our ears and freezing us in our place. I imagine an appearance on the road in front of us. *'What if day one was THE magical day?'*

At this moment, over two hours into the trek, I come to a realization. It is difficult to shift into a mountain mindset. The bombardment of billboards, social media apps, and noisy neighbors has been silenced. You stand in solitude in nature. It is you and your mind, and the scenery stripped free from city life and its distractions. The adjustment takes time. To be left alone with your senses is a shock to the system.

Because my senses are still dulled from normal city life, I have to use artificial means to ground myself. In time, I will be able to simply reside with my senses in silence; I have done this many times before in the mountains. For now, my mind takes creative license to continue imagining some magic. In my mind's eye, we see the snow leopard and walk side by side on the road.

Somehow, in this daydream, I suddenly possess uncanny abilities to speak with the snow leopard. As we walk, we discuss the harshness of the winter months. We discuss the latest human interactions and the latest population growth of leopards in the region. My guides and Radmir walk alongside, dumbfounded by this extraordinary turn of events. They walk in silence, admiring my ability to speak "snow leopard." It is a miraculous sighting never witnessed before.

Fast forward a year, and I am speaking at TED talks, conferences, libraries, and schools around the world, detailing the inexplicable walk-and-talk with the snow leopard. When my conversation with the snow leopard comes to an end on that fateful day, she bows her head to me and we touch, forehead to forehead. *'Pure lunacy. Oh, the things I dream up when up here in these mountainous fantasy worlds. Whatever, this trip is a child's dream, so let me dream like a child.'* I let out an audible, but soft, chuckle at myself.

 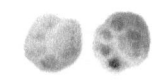

Just then, I stumble on a stone that jolts me back to my reality, slogging slowly up a narrow, barren path at the feet of the Himalayas. The daydream dissipates like a bubble's pop, leaving a faint mist in the air. I need to watch my step. Padma and Dorje cannot get the wrong idea about my abilities just because I am lost in my thoughts.

'If such magical experiences are beyond reality, what is possible then?' What will a sighting look like? Or feel like? If the trip is to turn auspicious, we will dare to partake in the tales of these cliffs. If only we are to be so fortunate. Probably, despite our efforts, we won't see the beauty. Only time will tell.' And so here I am again, lost in thought. It takes extreme effort to bring myself back to the present moment. The mind so easily slips away.

As we climb higher toward Rumbak, the peaks become thinner, more distinct, and increasingly jagged. Like towering monsters with overbearing arms and spears, they envelop us on all sides. The walkway narrows, sounds bouncing off each cliff side, and the cold becomes ever more concentrated in this tight space. I feel disoriented and slightly dizzy.

To keep my eyes on the nearby spaces and the immediate horizon, I work harder to find any signs of life. I find patches of green with little white flowers that dot the road, and I reach out and touch them. Dorje leans in and whispers, "These are called Kabra." They are intoxicatingly beautiful in this setting. I run a few past my nose. *'No smell, so either my olfactory system is frozen, or the flowers don't smell.'*

Regal, prickly patterns of ice form the edges of these white flowers' petals. This ice dusts the entire landscape. Hues of gray and sparkling ice spread out before us. In some places, moisture has stained the rocks burnt umber. These orange spots punctuate the scene with a stark, colored contrast.

The path narrows further, maybe two-and-a-half meters wide from cliff side to cliff side. I feel boxed in, and yet it feels fitting for a pathway up to the heavenly valleys I anticipate above us. *'A bottlenecked embrace from the mountains before being permitted to emerge into its glory above.'*

We continue walking in silence, in respect for this sacred space. Despite our efforts, our shuffling across loose scree sends a shattering cacophony of crunching sounds pitter-pattering along the pathway before us. It feels loud, like we are intruders in a place we do not belong.

The oppressive nature of these deep gully pathways brings upon us a real sense of smallness. I can imagine a drone flying up a few hundred meters directly overhead to reveal just how insignificant we seem, like puny dots in the immensity of the mountain range. '*We can no longer claim to be the masters of this domain. We are insignificant visitors, vagabonds. We humbly tread forward, honored to be allowed here.*' A real sense of nature's power overwhelms me.

In this moment, lurching out at my feet slithers a brownish-gray snake. Normally, I do not startle at snakes and generally love them. In the vastness and quiet of this space, however, where my eyes often turn upward, something darting at my feet with an aggressive hiss throws me off. I jump into the air, high-stepping and dancing out of the way. "My God, what was that?"

I look back at our guides, as the slender snake slinks away on the opposite side of the pathway. Padma chuckles, and Dorje smiles. "That is racer snake," Padma says.

Radmir chuckles, but he is a couple of steps in front of me and missed some of the moment. His movement must have started the snake across our path. My heart rate now hiked, I feel a rush of adrenaline and a fresh wave of energy.

Our group's collective noise continues to ricochet through this mini, pseudo-canyon as we creep further up into the mountains. With each step, we see something new, and it reminds us that this is home to some of the most precious fauna on the planet: Blue Sheep, Tibetan Wolf, Pallas Cat, Himalayan Ibex, Red Fox, Tibetan Sand Fox, Golden Eagle, Steppe Eagle, Ladakh Urial, Wild Yak, Pikas, Himalayan Lynx, Snow Leopard, and the aforementioned Ladakh Racer Snake, among many others.

Suddenly, another slight movement catches my eye. It is small and brownish gray, disappearing in lightning speed around a tiny rock. I barely catch a glimpse of its form, but it is slightly round. Seeing this

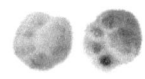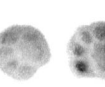

causes my heart to thump even faster, and I swallow to control the excitement. '*The first mammalian movement of the trip.*'

I stop walking and observe, studying the place of its disappearance. Our guides and Radmir also stop, taking cues from my abrupt cessation of walking along with my steady, quieted gaze in a singular direction.

At this moment, four people peer intensely at a forgotten edge of a rocky Himalayan road. We hear a squeak, and Dorje swings his hand up, cupping it to his ear. Padma flashes a knowing grin. "It is a pika," she says.

Radmir and my eyes dart here and there in a generally similar area. We cannot see anything. At the moment, the sounds of the animal matter more than sight, and they provide the necessary information to our guides.

Finally, she makes a shy appearance, poking her cute head out from behind a rock. All four of us delight in this sighting. I am close enough to see its rapid breaths, its upper chest heaving.

Glancing upward, I scour the sky above for fear of a winged predator watching nearby. She seems to be in the clear. '*Such a small creature in this vast space. How does something so miniature face off with Mother Nature herself and survive?*'

After a few minutes watching the tiny critter, we continue our rhythmic walking, taking in the haunting quiet of this place. Each step, every move of our clothing, creates an echo of sound behind us.

At this point, I become hyperaware of our disturbing presence in this space. I already knew it conceptually, but to actually feel it is something altogether different. To have your senses come back online and truly understand how our mere presence creates a significant break in the peace is remarkable. '*Sometimes perfection has to be disturbed to observe it. It reminds me of the Double Slit experiment, where the mere act of seeing disturbs the nature of things, collapsing possibility into reality. This is the ultimate disturbance.*'

Sometimes I imagine my thoughts to possess profundity, even though I know they are banal at best. No matter, I amuse myself and allow my wandering thoughts to continue.

'Heaven must feel more real here when we aren't here making noise. Maybe an entrance to heaven should be accompanied by silence and reverence. I always imagined the entrance to heaven to be boisterous and full of gaiety. Now, I wonder if the opposite is true. Why should the default be loud and obnoxious? Shouldn't the entrance to the divine be more serene and tranquil, much like this path I currently travel?'

I pull my mind back, forcibly, to the impressiveness of the here and now. With each step, the focus grows ever more present upon rhythm, pacing, breathing, foot placement, observing, listening, and feeling; all this is done with care and distinct intentionality.

While my mind wanders, I find my ability to re-center my attention improving with every meter of elevation we gain. Finally, after one grueling step after another, we arrive at the first home of the Rumbak valley, exhausted.

As we draw closer to the first home, the bend in the road opens to a gradually rolling hill up to a village of approximately twenty homes. The homes stand like heroes, carved into the history of the mountain, boasting prowess and power, and in possession of the most mythical tales.

The houses stand as evidence of man's relentless pursuit of greatness, of solitude, and of the divine. As in the Tower of Babel, human proclivity is to look up to the heavens, for better or for worse. It is our great trait and our fatal flaw.

This village stands as an ever-present defiance against the power of nature's glorious and spectacular wrath. Frozen winter after winter and scorching summer after summer, these homes, and people who prop them in their place, endure. I stand there at the feet of it all, out of breath.

"Astonishing. What a wild place. We're here. We made it," Radmir emits from behind his uneven breathing. "Now what?"

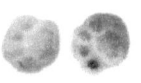

"Welcome to paradise, my friend," I muster enough vocal strength to mutter this something back to Radmir. Soft speaking is appropriate anyway, as I want to avoid disturbing the peace any more than I have already.

"Our home," smiles Padma. Her face beams brightly, and she holds the straps of her backpack on either side with her elbows pointed outward like an elementary child on the first day of school. She gently kicks a pebble to the side as a sort of physical re-acquaintance with this blessed ground.

"Our place, our home of beauty," echoes Dorje. They stand with such pride, gazing up at the village above. I think Dorje is from a neighboring village, but it seems he sees this place as his just the same.

Dorje and Padma flash glances at each other, an acknowledgement that they have accomplished something important yet again. They have dared to bring foreigners into their communities to share a bit of themselves with us. The sanctity of the moment is not lost on me.

I walk over and shake their hands, thanking them for bringing us to their home. Our many layers of gloves make the actual embrace awkward, but the gesture is clear: we respect and appreciate Dorje and Padma already. Radmir files in behind me and does the same.

"We think you will like this place very much. After a week or two, maybe." Dorje speaks with such conviction that his home will make such an impression on us. '*Could it be he sees us as teachable, as people willing to glean from this place?*'

Mountain ridges and peaks crowd in around this village from all sides. Car-sized boulders form a short wall that lines the pebbled road along the valley and up to the village homes.

We take in the view for a few minutes, breathless from what we see and from the laborious trek to this point into the clouds. We each set our bags down and sit on a rock that could double for a chair; the boulders in this space are giant.

The donkeys continue up toward the village. They seem to know exactly where they are going, even to the details of which individual home. Dorje gives them a loving pat on the back as they pass us.

In their efforts, my lungs feel powerless. I pant rapidly. It is like breathing with a heavy vest on your chest. Each breath feels like it achieves merely sixty percent of what I need. Despite my physical state, the all-encompassing and stupendous visual display enraptures me wholly. I am here in one of the most awe-inspiring "there" locations of my life.

After a few minutes, we gather ourselves and our belongings for the final push up to our homestay. We make our way along the gulley floor and finally arrive at the front gate of our home, our refuge for the next fourteen days. The front gate is enormous and painted bright red.

At this entrance, two beautiful people greet us. They are in their twilight years of life. The woman is bent over from what I can only imagine to be years of labor in this unforgiving world.

The man is bent over as well from a similar fate in life. *'Life at this elevation must be brutal. Beautiful and brutal.'* We exchange handshakes and names. Her name is Dahla, and his name is Palden. They nod graciously when they hear our names, Joshua and Radmir. Everything has to be translated because Radmir and I do not know Ladakhi.

I cannot help but think about my tattoo again. Here I am in this homestay deep in the Rumbak Valley. This is the most unexpected interconnectedness possible. *'I come from regular, small-town America. How is this the place where, and the people with whom, I will connect and seek wisdom? Who could have ever predicted this? How am I so blessed to have found this connection?'* Wonder rolls over me like a warm wine.

Turning to our guides, our hosts share a few words and then turn their attention back to us. Palden offers, through pantomime, to carry our backpacks and guide us to our room upstairs.

"No, it's okay, really," I suggest in protest. His hospitality and my willingness to accept win out. Radmir offers a similar protest to no avail. Palden lugs the heavy bags on his shoulders and leads the way upstairs. We follow behind him, and our guides file in behind us.

 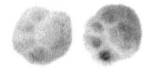

Palden drops off the bags and hurries back downstairs. Our hosts have limited English, maybe a few words at most. It seems our interactions with them will be somewhat limited. Or, we will have to find connections that transcend language. It depends on how much time we will spend in the house. *'I suspect our time inside the home will be limited to eating and sleeping only.'*

The room is spectacular. I lose my breath again, both from elevation and from sheer brilliance.

Our view from the third floor of this homestay stops me completely. I feel stuck in a statued state of awe.

To be clear, I have walked on the rim of Kilimanjaro, Mount Kenya, and Mount Kinabalu. From a treehouse thirty meters in the sky, I have observed the canopy of the Costa Rican rainforest. I have enjoyed the backdrop sparkle of the Ionian Sea from an ancient theatre in Taormina with fresh, cool cannoli on my tongue. I have seen the San Juan Islands from the cockpit eye of a Beechcraft Baron on several occasions. I have explored the Kyzylkum desert in Uzbekistan atop a spunky camel. I have flown over the Grand Canyon in a glass-bottom helicopter. I have tasted the salty air on the Maltese shoreline from the top of a flyboard, three meters in the air. I sat four yards from a powerful tigress in Bandhavgarh. In the night, I have walked with wild lions a mere three meters away. I have observed holiday festivities from the home of the Pa' Lungan tribe.

And yet, none of these compares to this view from a homestay window in frosty Rumbak at the feet of the snow leopard's throne. I sit and soak. *'What do I smell? What do I hear? What do I see when I open my eyes?'* I am dumbstruck.

After some time, I pull back my gaze from the outside and turn my attention to the interior of the room. Large, lattice-style windows stretch from floor to ceiling and circle the entire room, offering a view of God's mountainous playground before us.

Naturally, these windows welcome, with open arms, the unadulterated crisp air as well, with no insulation for the weary traveler. "Any water bottles, cameras, or other valuables will have to remain inside our blankets with us if they have a fighting chance to avoid being a frozen brick by morning's call," I suggest.

Radmir nods in agreement. He stands in awe, taking in the view and the moment. We stand there, motionless. I reach over and pinch my arm, literally. I need to know this is real. A real "there" experience, the kind I will tell as a tale to my children.

Radmir and I share more in this moment than we ever could in one hundred ordinary conversations. This shared moment transcends language. My fingers twitch, either from the excitement of the pending fourteen days, or from the chill, or from a mixture of both.

A pattern of multi-colored rugs from all across Central Asia forms a dizzying display across the ground. They overlap with each other and create layers of physical separation from the chilled floor itself. Much like the entire experience to this point, the carpets merely punctuate the stimulating senses-on-fire experience.

There are insets in the concrete walls. *'I'm certain Dahla and Palden placed these here, with care and intention.'* In these spaces, snow leopard figurines, crafted by women in the village, have been carefully placed. Alongside these decorations are candles and pictures of the Dalai Lama. There are prayers framed and resting against the wall. These sensorial spaces in the room contribute to the flavor, texture, and variety in an already-overwhelming visual exhibit. Our room offers a playground for the senses.

Once again, my mind wanders in this grand wilderness. *'Where are all the social media influencers for this view? Where are all the duck-faced selfie photos? A little frost scares you all away? What, you need a beach? You need a fancy infinity pool and overpriced caviar, do you?'*

Sometimes, when I find myself in the unimaginable and enchanted places off the well-worn tourist path, I resort to a bit of self-righteous mockery. I amuse myself, happy to have found a place unspoiled by a clickbait travel vlogger. A few inner, snarky comments are all it takes to crack a smile on the left side of my mouth and to truly appreciate this special place.

 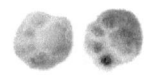   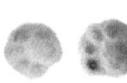

After some twenty minutes or so, I jostle myself out of my stunned stupor. Radmir does the same. We move in silence because there is nothing to say. To utter words is to diminish the experience, to interrupt perfection.

I walk the perimeter of the room, inspecting every viewpoint out into the snowy jungle before us. At our feet, along the perimeter, are the bed spaces on opposite sides of this spacious room.

Eventually, I make my way to the door and walk down a hallway and out toward the balcony. A gust of bone-chilling wind slaps me in the face. I notice Radmir follows close behind me as a co-inspector.

"This is wild. Are we really here?" Radmir whispers. The rhetorical question still feels like a genuine question because our reality has not fully settled within us. Energy boils inside both of us. This excitement, mixed with the cold, causes our voices to flutter in unstable tones. I can hardly utter a controlled word.

"I can't even make sense of all this," I whisper back. There is no point speaking beyond a whisper. Already, our soft words shatter the silence and the ambiance of the ghost's domain. But we have to speak; we are compelled, both of us, to acknowledge the unbelievable element of everything around us.

Too often, words like "awesome" are bandied about and used with futility. This time, these words fit the bill. '*When the words that describe something awesome actually match something of awe, something to remember until the grave, you know you've lived beautifully.*' Heaven is here.

The rooftop balcony space resides just outside our bedroom, and we venture out, braving the temperatures and weaponized breeze, just to see everything, unobstructed by windows. Puffs of breath swirl around our nostrils, and my cheekbones and fingertips ache within seconds.

This roof space is quite large and spans to another room on the other side of the house. I feel compelled to remain here no matter how frigid. Much like this entire fantastic village, I want to stand in defiance to see what others cannot endure to see. '*I will see this place at any cost. What is the state of cold? Is it not just a state of feeling to be overcome?*' I can almost hear ghostly whispers whipping in the wind and chanting my name. '*Home. Home.*'

Once again, I remember my tattoo and the Eternal Knot; I am now forever tied to this place. I remember the concept of the duality of reality; I think about the warmth of the people and the death chill of the air. I think about the gray ghost and her divinity and the death-defying climbs it will take to see her.

In my peripheral vision, I notice Radmir transfixed in thought, lost in the sights of the hills and mountains in front of us. We are children lost in a wonderland, lost in the magnificence of the impossible.

Gently interrupting the moment, Dahla appears in the doorway of the balcony and beckons us down to the main living room for an early dinner. I welcome the thought of human warmth and food that can stave off hypothermia. My entire body rattles with chill already, fingers purple and teeth chattering. Tomorrow morning's work will begin in the dark before daylight wakes. An early dinnertime followed by an early bedtime makes sense to me.

We gather for the meal. The space where we will eat glimmers in sparkling silver and candlelight. I squint from the intense brilliance. We had just come from a sunset where the sky was slightly dimmed, gray and white. From that, we then walked into a dark stairwell and finally into shimmering luminance, all within a few seconds. The intense contrasts prove harsh on the eyes.

Silver cups, bowls, jugs, and plates fill and surround the entire interior. Again, Radmir and I stand in awe, unable to utter words. '*What a dazzling display. Stupidly beautiful,*' I think to myself.

We sit together in a circle on the ground around the central fireplace. Both Dorje and Padma enter the room. "It is called 'chu-thang,'" mentions Padma, referring to the fireplace. We gather and sit on large pillows. Generous portions of steaming hot soups, creamy steaming potatoes, and tender beef are served alongside large portions of soft, warm bread. My soul is encouraged with this meal. I feel a renewed sense of the possible.

45

Soon enough, our conversation veers toward tales of snow leopard sightings. These stories titillate the ears while soup warms our hands, shivering the body back to life.

Snow leopard tales, grown gargantuan with hyperbolic additions over the years, appropriately align with the bursting exaggeration of candlelight off the silver pans and plates. If there is one candle, there might as well be twenty from the reflections and augmentations of the plateware. Tonight, they have at least 400 candles lit. We eat aglow in literal and figurative light. It is a near-abstract experience. And yet, this is the most grounded, sensory experience in my life.

Dorje laughs fully, a burst of energy and excitement in the eyes, bread in hand, and a bowl of soup in the other. Padma smiles gently and leans over her bowl, sipping her soup. Radmir asks Dorje another question, and the conversation rolls on.

Occasionally, Padma adds the perfect anecdote to the tale Dorje shares, adding a layer of genuine human emotion to the plot. "That was when our guests cried. Snow leopard was special thing for them to see. She finally see it. She searched for many years but never see." Padma beams with joy and satisfaction. "Maybe you both will see her. She whispers. If we are lucky, we will catch her passing shadow."

I lean in closely. Radmir does the same. Hundreds of candles cast monstrous shadows and highlights across our faces. As each story reaches its climax, we crouch closer to the center of the circle. We grow quiet and speak in whispers, almost out of fear, or respect, of the gray ghost. Eventually, each tale grows back into a crescendo of excitement and volume. A feast for the senses. Our eyes expand wildly in the candlelight.

The room's energy remains high throughout the early evening. A mixture of hope, determination, excitement, and real fear mix together in our first night's discussion. *'I imagine this laughter and energy will echo into the night in my ears long after we've all gone to bed.'* My heart, head, and stomach feel as full as ever.

After dinner and before bed, Radmir and I venture outside and briskly scamper around the Rumbak Village. Full darkness is soon, but we have just enough time to adventure about. We want to lay eyes on the surroundings before we start our arduous work in the morning.

The labyrinth of walkways leading to and from various houses intrigues and mystifies. Every turn and corner offers a view of a beautiful home and another collection of dogs, cows, donkeys, and yaks. Many homes have a separate space designated for the livestock and skulls mounted above the wooden entrance gate.

Surrounding each home, we see multicolored prayer flags on bridges, fences, and roofs. Wind throws these bright red, green, blue, white, and yellow flags mercilessly about. They represent peace, compassion, strength, and wisdom. At least this is what I read before coming on the trip. Foreigners often know of these flags from K2 and Everest documentaries. But for the local communities, these flags hold significant meaning and power; they are not mere decorations.

Occasionally, a local resident, dressed in thick layers, saunters past us and offers a cheerful "Jullay" in the deep dusk of the evening. Most people's clothes are brown or black. Nothing flashy. I can never quite make out their actual physical figure; the layers of clothes are so thick that they form a general shape of a human. Everyone walks around in this same, bloated form.

The remaining blue-gray daylight fades, and the landscape turns a dark blue. We can make out a few stars against the darkening canopy. Radmir asks, "You ready for tomorrow?" A billowing plume of steam simultaneously moves from his mouth and temporarily disguises his face.

I nod, too numb to speak. *'I think I'm ready. I hope I'm ready. What the hell is tomorrow going to look like anyway? How do I know if I'm ready? This is why I venture into these places to see if I can be a part of a place like this. To see if I'm really ready. Sometimes, just to see.'*

Eventually, as complete darkness descends on us, we find our way back to the homestay and gather around the fireplace "chu-thang" again. We thrust our hands toward the fire until steam coils off our fingers. *'No one understands the cold until they've been here. I remember watching documentaries on Yakutia. Is it really that much colder than here? I used to live in Belarus, and we'd laugh about our temperatures being regularly colder than those in Siberia. But here?*

Oh, it's colder here.' With some hot tea and cookies to sustain us for the night, we make our way upstairs. On my way to the room, I use the bathroom for the first time, and what a surprise.

There is a hole. That is all. Just a glacially chilled room, with a dirt floor, and a half-meter hole in the middle of it all. I feel grateful that there is a bathroom at all, and that it is in a private space, but I am also shocked.

The fact that it is a hole is not what shocks me. Having traveled around the world in unique places, finding bathrooms in various villages has been my norm. I am used to going into the backyard among the chickens, stepping inside the outhouse, floorboards bouncing unsteadily beneath me, and using the "hole."

No, what shocks me is that this same setup is deemed appropriate for temperatures that can freeze your urine midstream. '*You mean to tell me that in this hellish cold I am to bear it all and squat? My American rump can't handle this. I'll freeze to death most embarrassingly. I'm too pampered for this.*' I crack a smile at my own entitled silliness.

The world, for centuries, lived in ways that Westernized folks could never imagine. Our memory is fickle, if not absent and ignorant altogether. Medieval realities would destroy most of us. We mostly know the coddling of modernization. Even the poorest and sickest among us live like kings and queens compared to humanity's past. A mere cellphone in our hands separates us from the past. Any king would have given up his entire kingdom for one cellphone.

Quickly, I get over myself and take care of business. '*If the danger of freezing to death is possible, you do not need hours on the throne with a device in hand. When the cold can pierce you in your most vulnerable places, a bathroom trip is as brief as a hungry man's prayer before dinner.*'

The first night in the homestay brings a disruption to the body. The biting chill inside our room seeps into my core and taunts my mental strength. We light a fire in the fireplace in the center of our room. The fuel is dried cow dung; this proves a resourceful option when trees are sparse.

This fire is short-lived, though. We feel the temptation of warmth for only four or five minutes. This is our final heated indulgence before it is "lights out" and the freeze creeps over us with its talons like an evil spirit.

We go to opposite sides of the room and choose our beds among the options offered. We already understand that nothing escapes the cold in this room. Radmir claims his corner, and I grab mine. These will be our frozen beds for our frozen fourteen days. *'If hell is hot, then this must be a special version of heaven.'*

I bury myself under six layers of blankets. Under normal circumstances, this would be hellish heat torture. Here and now, under these six layers, I can barely find enough warmth for sleeping. I scoot my camera and batteries to my waist on my left side, under all the blankets, and place my water bottle in the same position but on my right-hand side.

I feel squished under the weight and boxed in by my gear on both sides. After about thirty minutes, I feel a tinge of warmth rolling across my body and realize sleep may be a possibility after all.

My mind wanders to the moments of the day. One thing stands out: the word "hospitality" belittles the treatment we have received at the hands of our hosts and others within the community. It is now an insufficient word.

The people of Ladakh define, for me, a new standard of excellence in hospitality. The food, the conversations, the love, the gear, the care taken with lodging, the freedom to explore, the forgiveness of our accidentally intrusive behaviors, the inspirational ideas, and the general welcome all envelop us.

As usual, this place holds extreme opposites, warmth from the people and cold that can kill. *'This is my first taste of what it feels like to live here with the Ladakhi people of the Rumbak valley.'* With these thoughts rumbling in my mind, I fall fast asleep.

50

Chapter 2:

Struggle & Search

At 5:00 am, we wake against everything sane. In defiance of all biological commands, we rise. Like standing up once again during a cage battle with a tiger as blood pours from each eye socket and every muscle fiber cries for mercy. The cage is our icy room, and the battle is the night's menacing, relentless punches of brutal, frozen frost to the face. My throat screams in crusted agony.

Everything feels stiff. I muscle my blankets off me and collect my camera, batteries, and water bottle. *'I wonder if this is what it's like moving around in space; everything is so impossible right now. My brain tells appendages to move, but the delay and the actual speed at which I'm moving are so slow. Everything labors at a snail's pace.'* This is heaven.

The first order of business is to gather the layers needed for the day. *'Is there anything I need to supplement my current bedtime clothes?'* I decide to start with what I have on instead of stripping to the first layer and risking a breakfast of hypothermia.

I add one more layer of socks to the two already on my feet. I add two, thick sweaters and one summit jacket. I add one green trekking pant. Finally, I gather my summit glove to layer on top of my current liner glove. Radmir moves mechanically in the opposite corner, fighting to complete the same task.

Next, Radmir and I both begin collecting our gear for the day. Batteries, tripods, extra shoelaces, trekking poles, and head torches are just a few of the items I collect in the darkness. I move every finger with aching pain and physical resistance.

Suddenly, I detect a patch of shadows hovering, or lurking, in the upper right-hand corner of the room. I struggle to make out what it is, and everything is still so dark at this ungodly hour of the morning. Despite the blackout of our room, only partially lit by our faces glowing from cell

 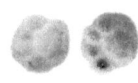

phone screens, I see slight extensions of this darkness expanding out onto the ceiling like veins. My already-slow movements halt in the haunting awareness.

Rubbing my eyes, I attempt to readjust my sight. It fails. The same presence of darkness in the far corner persists. I blink; still there. I grunt to my feet and stumble a few steps closer in the lightless room. No change. Just a slight tint of darkness deeper than the dimness already filling the room. *'What the hell is that? How can I imagine this? Am I this messed up this morning?'*

I see it move a bit, like a pulse or jitter. The movement gradually slinks along the wall up to where it meets the ceiling. I jump back a step and gasp sharply. Radmir hears my scuffle and asks, blindly, "What's wrong? You okay?"

"Yeah. No, no, I'm fine. Thought I saw something." Hallucinations at this elevation and in this shivering room are the only rational rationale, so I appease his concern with my confident response. I simply startled from something not really there.

But I did see something. I still see it now, pulsating. A mass of molasses-like substance latched to the wall and ceiling, yet nearly hovering, separate from the wall. *'What in the hell?'* I softly mutter to myself, trying not to alarm Radmir.

It just hangs there like smog snagged to the ceiling, unable to escape, screaming for release. Possibly, I have projected my feelings into my visible plane. After all, it is relatively gloomy in here this brutal morning, and I am wrestling with the demons of the cold, trying to will my body into movements.

Whatever I see must be symptoms of slight insomnia and insanity from the skin-tingling chill of our room. *'Whatever. Who has time to entertain imaginary demonic blobs of darkness when the cold is a formidable enough foe?'*

I shrug it off and walk back over to my bags and resume my packing for the day. As I pull out my trekking poles, my mind fixates upon that dark space on the wall. *'Is it an animal? What animal has that shape? Why did it move?'*

I sit there befuddled, but with a face too frozen to show it. Radmir continues to pack, unaware of the opaque spectacle and my reactionary angst. I take another look up. Nothing but some faint, normal shadows now. '*I knew I was making it up in my head. It's just a damned shadow.*' To find the source of these shadows, I swivel my head around. The shadows seem to be cast from an outside light against the window curtains.

The morning's light, having now crept in, brings clarity and fades away any worries of my earlier fears. I reason with myself: '*It was nothing. Just a simple aberration from the interplay of light and shadows.*' I shove in some packaged snacks for the day and grip my head torch.

Lastly, I grab my camera. It pulls heavily on me, but I force it to my side. It is too fragile to lug around inside my backpack. Besides, I might see something at any moment out there, and the camera has to be ready. I have to be ready.

Packed thick with layers of clothes and heavy bags weighing down on our shoulders, we emerge from the room. The ceilings are short, and the wall width is thin. Additionally, we are a bit wobbly this first morning. I can hear our bags scraping the walls, and I see Radmir knock his head on the ceiling as he descends the stairs.

We exit our homestay, following our swift-moving guides. Padma leads, and Dorje walks behind us. Dorje seems to be gauging our abilities on this first, frosty trek. He peers ahead with beady eyes in the pre-dusk dim, watching our steps, our breathing, and our pace.

Already, a few steps out into the village, we slip on icy rocks. First, I slip to the right and catch myself with my left boot on a patch of dry pebbles. My trekking poles stabilize my upper body once I stab them into the ground.

Then, Radmir slips, hands whirling in helicopter circles as he struggles to regain his balance. He steadies himself just before landing backwards. Both of us have some immediate adjustments to make.

As we emerge, the landscape and mountain ridge sprawl out in front of us like a painting coming to life in 3-D. What had been our mere view the day before is now our physical reality with very real rewards and

 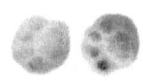

dangers. We now become the actors dancing on stage as opposed to the audience members taking it in from comfortable seats.

For those unfamiliar with wildlife spotting or research, the question might be, 'Why wake at such a Godless hour of the morning?' Each wildlife project demands varying strategies and time periods for work. I have worked through the night, trekking aardvarks and caracals, sleeping only in the daytime. I have busied myself under the unforgiving sun, preparing meat for cheetahs at a rehabilitation and rewilding center. Context matters.

For us, the sole purpose of this morning's scamper is to scope the towering peaks and deep gulleys to determine the rest of our day's work in the field. We need to do a pre-breakfast scouring of the landscape to collect data and chart our strategy for the day, be it in one valley and ridgeline or another. Nature decides our plan, and we listen to her carefully.

We depart from the homestay village and enter the official edge of the playpen for freaks like us. We now ascend into the glorious Himalayas that surround the homestay, a homestay already deep in the mountains.

I feel the intensity of the trip immediately and suck air as rapidly as possible. My heart rate beats rapidly, and my lungs beg for more air. *'Is that sweat under my balaclava? In these temps? How is it possible to outwork Nature's frozen air and work up a sweat?'*

I glance over at Radmir, who slowly trudges about four meters behind me. His violent breathing pushes puffs far out beyond his face. His eyes betray him, revealing an intense physical struggle, even though most of his face is covered by his balaclava.

Beyond our breaths and crunching steps on frozen rocks, all else is silent in this blue-gray, icy morning. A hint of daylight tickles the horizon line of peaks.

I look ahead at Padma and back at Dorje. Padma and Dorje both wear camouflage green and brown trousers and camouflage jackets. They each have black liner gloves and camouflage hats.

Every one of their steps pushes forward, methodically and forcefully, with little restraint. No weakness or tremors show in their bodies. Despite their stalwart presence, puffs of condensation emanate from their balaclavas. All four of us eject white clouds about our heads. *'We must look like a train crossing the Himalayas, puff of steam and one train car after another in a perfect line along the ridgeline.'*

What consumes me is the quiet. The gelid and silent mix together, pirouetting through my lungs and ears. The sound of breath and the scuffle of my steps are all the sounds permitted in this deadening and deafening terrain.

Everything also feels fragile. I feel like the mere sound of stepping on an old, dry branch would shatter the landscape, catalyzing multiple avalanches at once. The frigid pressure is so strong that it seems even the rocks might snap with a "crack" and break into a filet of sharp shards. Or a strong enough shout might bring the whole thing to the ground in pieces, like a bowling ball crashing into a chest made of glass.

I perceive a crackling and delicate environment, but the reality is a colossal, indomitable, solid whitewashed playground where the snow leopard cuddles its cubs under the warmth of its massive tail. My perception and the reality of this heaven both overlap and clash.

As my mind wanders with each step, I am reminded of the silence again. *'I would think this silence would invite me to meditate. In actual fact, I'm plagued with anxiety; this is a deafening silence I've never experienced.'* I have explored plenty of backcountry trails without any semblance of civilization in sight. I have wandered for days on end without any human contact, much to my contentment.

However, this is a different level of solitude. I am with three others, but I might as well have been dropped off in the farthest northern Canadian territories, alone. The nothingness, the emptiness of anything auditory, becomes my companion. My balaclava wraps my ears, further stifling sound. I am bottled up and turn further inward, inside my head.

When we arrive at the end of this morning's short walk to begin studying the mountainside, I find myself unsteady. To regulate myself, I sit down, place my day pack behind me, and lie back against it, positioning my

 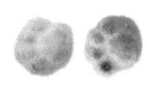

body at a forty-degree angle. For further stability, I raise my knees up near my chest.

As a result of these interventions, my breath slowly returns to a normal rate, and my heart's rapid rhythms calm. *'This will take some getting used to for sure.'* The respite on the ground soothes.

Out comes my fifteen-pound camera-and-lens combination. I carry a Nikon D750 and a Sigma 150-600mm. It is my burden in this unforgiving place. But I must see everything, and I must participate in each moment by choosing to frame the story of this adventure through my creative eye. This necessity requires a robust camera and lens, and all its collective weight.

When I work with my camera in this place, I remove my outer summit glove from my left hand. I need more dexterity and precision, and the summit glove restricts me. The elements bite at my fingers even with a liner glove still on my hand. I can only last a few minutes. *'God forbid I have to keep this glove off for too long; my fingers might freeze.'*

I rotate between glove-on-and-watching and glove-off-with-camera. The delicate dance between frostbite and rest begins, as does the balance between seeing behind the lens and just seeing.

I position my camera on the bridge of my left eye and use it as a scope. Aiming up to examine the landscape, I rest the body of my large lens on top of my knees. My camera's crosshairs lock in on a faraway ridgeline, and I begin tracing along the horizon, up and down and up and down.

My shivering fingers rattle and unsteady my pan. Consequently, the view from the viewfinder jolts and loses focus every few meters of investigation. Still, I persist and keep working at it until my fingers begin cooperating. I learn to lean into the stiffness and bend my fingers to my will.

Radmir stands a few meters away, wrestling with his own camera setup, fighting the elements bravely. He remains standing, shifting his position every few seconds. Like me, he uses the camera as a pseudo-scope, panning ridgelines and gulleys.

Meanwhile, our guides station themselves somewhat near each other, about ten meters apart, scopes pointed in opposite directions, continuously pivoting and searching. They know what to look for and how to see it. As professional guides in these mountains, they can spot anything, no matter how hidden. It is their superpower. This power is essential out here in this wintry whiteout.

The snow leopard is the queen of hiding in plain sight. One can stand five meters away and still not spot her, let alone from a kilometer away. She is an enigma, invisible to us.

The snow leopard can see us. She has special eyes. There is no camouflage we can muster to escape her view. Padma and Dorje, successful as they are as guides, must be able to tap into extraordinary skills to help us all see what is normally impossible to see.

What helps is that our stated purpose is to see the gray ghost. You often see what you aim at. With laser focus, our odds of a sighting increase.

I glance back over at Dorje and Padma. Dorje looks up from his scope and sees me looking his way. He waves at me and throws a "thumbs up" sign, barely perceptible with his thick, heavy gloves. *'Wait, a snow leopard?'*

He returns the brow of his head to the top edge of the sight on his scope and pivots to look in another direction. *'No snow leopard. He's just checking in on me. I have to figure out what their signal will be if they see one.'*

Dorje and Padma seem impervious to the bone-chilling air. It almost feels like the act of seeing, of searching, is enough adrenaline-induced warmth to distract their minds from external circumstances.

They are titans, holding their positions, rock solid and intensely focused on this morning's reconnaissance mission. Their "get-on-with-it" and focused dispositions exemplify consummate professionalism.

This is business. It is serious work. They hold the ultimate respect for this mountain and this animal. Last night's tales showcased this. We are only a few hours into our time with these two people, and yet every choice, every movement, every carefully chosen word is evidence of their competence and dedication.

 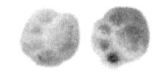

'*I want to be like Padma and Dorje. I want to see what they see. Furthermore, I aspire to show their level of strength.*' I dream of a life where I have developed some competence approximating theirs, and I have the distinct honor of guiding people into the heavens to see the ghost. A movie of me accomplishing this runs across my mind's eye.

Suddenly, both Padma and Dorje swivel their scopes in the same direction. The abrupt movement pulls me out of my daydreaming.

They have real scopes. Padma holds a Swarovski Optik BTX 95. Dorje works with a Zeiss Conquest Gavia 85. As a result, they can see better than we can. These tools combine with their years of experience into a powerful combination.

Conversely, Radmir and I are like toddlers working on a power grid with toy hammers. We act like mere children in the face of our guides' experience, strength, and knowledge. I stop scanning for a short period and study them out of respect; I owe them my attention. They remain locked, looking in the same direction as before.

My eyes brighten and my heartbeat surges once again. '*Have they spotted something? Are we onto the snow leopard already?*' After a few minutes, their scopes diverge, and they return to their usual scanning. '*False alarm. Whatever they saw doesn't seem to matter. I hope this isn't the way it goes for the whole trip because my heart can't take this constant excitement.*'

Dorje's approach is more of a pan and lock, pan and lock, pan and lock. He moves across a space and then freezes, examining one space for a time. He establishes a rhythm right away. Meanwhile, Padma methodically scours spaces with her scope, a few meters at a time. Unlike Dorje, she scans in a continuous flow, without any pauses or resets.

A few meters from me, Radmir holds my Nikon Coolpix P1000. I remember debating with myself at the Kenmore Camera shop as to which camera would fit the bill best for this trip. '*Yes, this Coolpix is a weird option, but the reach, whether the sensor is small or not, is perfect. For capturing quality videos of a distant snow leopard, regardless of any compression distortion or heat haze, this could be my best bet.*'

I return to searching along with the others. Hoisting the heavy camera and lens up into place, I pick a point and start exploring within a few meters of that initial starting spot. Radmir and I mimic our guides and point in different directions. '*Mimicry is the most flattering praise.*'

Again, I notice the silence. Our team has not spoken a mere whisper for at least an hour now. No noise pollution. No trains, airplanes, horns, or city clattering. No village animals out on the prowl, growling or barking. As for the wild animals, they move in stealth, so we would not hear them anyway. There is a void of noise.

Occasionally, the wings of a distant crow disrupt the emptiness and make helicopter-like bursts of sound ripple across the sky, interrupting our serene scene. Any sounds at all, no matter how subtle, jar us out of the tranquility of the moment. '*Really, some day when I try to explain this experience to people, words will fail me.*'

Padma and Dorje study, undeterred by any disruptive sounds. They peer into each layout of land, trying to perceive any evidence of the snow leopard's presence.

I notice the weight of my lens bearing down on me. Dropping it to my right side and rubbing my right arm tempts blood flow to return. For the first time, I feel a tingling and numbness in that arm.

Also, I notice my stomach's morning growl, and my breath is lighter and shallower in hushed anticipation. Steam ebbs in and out of my balaclava. Everything feels like a sort of meditation, with awareness of the present keeping my attention.

I decide to rehearse my knowledge of snow leopard searching. What constitutes evidence of snow leopards? The possibilities are endless.

Is there a group of circling vultures? That would be a likely kill and a place to investigate after breakfast.

Is there an obvious kill in plain sight? That would be a necessary area to explore.

Are there prints anywhere within eyesight to track later in the day, provided there is no fresh snow falling? Are there territorial scratches or urine marks anywhere? How about scat? Do we see any anti-predator behavior from any other animals, such as rapid movement from a herd of blue sheep?

And what about those blue sheep? Are they gathering in any space to graze? They may be a certain target for a snow leopard's afternoon snack.

What about auditory clues? Do we hear any warning calls from birds or mammals, territorial or otherwise? Where are the humans in this space, if any at all? The snow leopards will avoid these areas, and so should we.

Only Padma and Dorje know the latest circular routes of the leopards. Snow leopards hunt and mate across large territories, often circling back on previous routes. Our guides have all the data stored in their heads.

I recall my time working in the Naliboki Forest with Zoologist and world-renowned researcher Vadim Sidorovich. His work has been critical in the aftermath of the Chernobyl disaster. This was my more formal training in wildlife tracking and research.

He always kept me abreast of what we were doing and the latest findings. I was never in the dark with him. His wealth of knowledge and up-to-date data would point us in our day-to-day work.

However, here in these humongous Himalayas, I feel blind and a bit helpless in my ignorance and our non-conversive approach. I feel limited in how I can help.

Even with our guides' skills and professionalism, sightings will be difficult. Usually, tourists search for snow leopards from February to April. This timeframe is generally mating season. Weather conditions are more favorable. The male calls from the ridges, and his haunting screeches echo and bound across the vertical mountainous halls.

This behavior aids in successful sightings for snow leopard aficionados. The snow leopard's silhouetted form appears against the evening blue sky on ridgelines. The tourists gasp and scamper to their cameras. Shutters clap continuously in bursts and flutters. Quiet cheers, fists in the air, and muffled chatter fill the small crowd.

'*How glad I am to be alone with my team. I would hate to be in such a crowd for an experience like this.*' I remind myself why I am grateful for this trip of seclusion and wilderness.

However, without the extra eyes and feet, sightings are more difficult. During mating season, with a crew of fifty or so tourists at one time, the teams can split up into multiple valleys and share findings with each other via radio.

If one group finds a snow leopard, the other groups join if the situation allows. The opportunity to spot a snow leopard is exponentially more probable. It is a game of numbers, and the more you have, the greater the chance for sightings.

I chose a time of year that is colder and more challenging. Why? '*Because I don't want any tourists around me with their annoying coughs, whispered chattering, coffees in hand, and their general neediness. No, like in my childhood, I want the mountain mostly to myself. Radmir is a perfect partner with his strength and muted reflection, and our guides are like mountain spirits, leading us toward divinity. Other than these dear people, I don't want to be stuck with the annoying gaze of others.*' I want only the gaze of the ghost and my chance to gaze back. Sartre would be proud of me.

Once again, I find my mind wandering in this intoxicating place. I pull myself back again to help in the scanning process. Every time I lose focus, the camera finds its way back to my side.

We stay out here in the blistering, icy air until the sun peaks over the horizon. We watch in amazement as the sun finally makes an appearance in this early morning and creates spear-like shadowed peak outlines across mountain faces on the opposite side of the range. Despite the sun's rays, everything feels like ice, looks like ice, and literally is ice in this slippery-smooth and jaggedly-sharp wilderness.

'*Well, look at that. The sun acts as its own projector and splashes one mountain's majestic pinnacles onto the face of a mountain on the other side of this glorious region. Amazing!*' I cannot hold back these invasive inner thoughts with each new breathtaking experience.

Every few minutes, I find myself lost again in thought. The enveloping chilly landscape serves to bring my numbed body into a trance-like state, further aiding in my proclivity toward meditation and daydreaming. Sometimes, I just let myself go and enjoy the ride, losing a grip on consciousness in the death-inviting freeze. To let go is to seek freedom.

The stark shadow display slowly descends to the base of the opposing mountain until the sun is more directly overhead, and the shadows disappear altogether. The entire topography takes on another set of hues and life.

Warm colors now control and paint the landscape. Shadows give way to an orange glow beaming off of snowcapped peaks. What was a transparent and white frozen stream is now a sparkling streak of bluish ice, reflecting colors from the sky above, as a patch of sky bravely peeks through the dense clouds. Our eyes delight in this feast for the senses.

I collect time-lapse videos of the phenomenon. The appearance of the sun, while glorious, offers a tease of warmth. There is only a negligible difference in temperature. Sun, or no sun, the frosty air hammers away at us, pecking at our stamina and determination.

After about three hours of data collection from the first morning's reconnaissance mission, we return to the homestay to defrost around a hearty breakfast. The return to the home is a fifty-minute scamper back up the sprawling hill.

Along the way, we notice ancient petroglyphs carved into stones. They are aligned along the pathway, intentionally. They reside beside the road to bring a sense of connectedness between the ancient past and the present.

There is a oneness that is palpable as a result of these remarkable carvings. Once again, I feel the urge to glance at my Eternal Knot tattoo. A sense of awe comes across me, even warming my body. Here I am now a connected part of this place, this "there" place.

Buddhist, cultural, and ancient in nature, the carvings compel us to wonder on ages of wisdom and enlightenment, of pain and triumph, of tradition and family, of community and unity, of choosing beauty and embracing it no matter the consequences.

Similar to my time in the market in Leh, I choose to keep the camera at my side. I feel that these must be seen only in person. Taking a photograph seems like a disrespectful act, even though our guides allow us. As a result, the burden of holding up the camera is abated for a short while.

"These writings are very important to us. Before we go to breakfast, let us share with you a little something." Dorje explains the history of these writings and symbols. Some are prayers. Some are histories. Some are symbols of our practices in the past. He shares how their entire lives, in one form or another, can be understood through these ancient markings.

Padma watches with furled eyebrows and genuine intent. Her usual jovial and lighthearted tones are subdued. Dorje continues on, sharing their histories with us. Radmir and I listen carefully.

After about ten minutes of opening up such revered and sensitive cultural information, Dorje finishes, slightly bows toward us, and then motions toward the homestay for breakfast. Our hearts and heads are full; now we go to fill our stomachs.

As we inch ever closer to the homestay, an elderly woman carrying firewood in a wicker basket passes us and grins warmly, her body bent under the weight of the basket full of wood.

A few minutes later, a farmer passes by with several Himalayan yaks, beginning a precarious ascent up the opposite side of the ridge for advantageous grazing in snowless pockets.

Cows sound off at us as we pass by their home. Crows caw overhead and swirl in dizzying displays. A dog trots by, dodging and weaving through the maze of homes swiftly, clearly in search of a warm place and food.

Dung patties sit in window frames outside each home, left there to dry and later provide fuel for fires. The pitter-patter flapping of the prayer flags atop each house claps in approval to everything our senses perceive.

Back in the homestay, a heaping breakfast consists of steaming eggs, bread, and porridge. I salivate at the meal. Each salty, warm bite soothes me from the inside and uplifts my weary body.

We warm our hands on hot chocolate in teacups and sip in any calories we can for the day's pending extreme terrain and climbing. A few extra cookies and assorted nuts do the trick.

At just past nine in the morning and with our bellies full from breakfast, Padma peeks her head in the room and motions for us to prepare to depart for the day. Our guides pack lunches and any other necessities in the hallway. They operate quietly, with a steely calm and gentle presence about them.

This is our first day, our first journey into the impressive peaks above us. Our first opportunity to begin studying, listening, and understanding the ways of a Ladakhi wildlife tracker, the Rumbak valley's spirit, the geography of this region of the Himalayas, and the snow leopard herself.

We step out of the house to witness the delight of an earlier-morning village that was inaudible to now a cozy community bright with energy. A group of young children plays in the snow. They occupy a space between six houses where the snow has been tamped down into a mini skating rink.

They have sleds of sorts made from scrap sheets of metal and rope. Two small girls grab one together, run, and then leap together into a slide, eventually careening into a little pile of snow at the other side of the makeshift "rink."

Suddenly, a pounding bang startles me just above my head. I see a woman on her roof clearing the gutter. She wields a hammer and teeters on a ladder. The ladder extends from her balcony, a balcony not unlike the one in our homestay. From her extension, she can reach up to the roof. *'So much energy at this time of the morning. I like it here. Do we really have to march out? Can't we stay here a while and soak all this in?'*

Across the way, an old man emerges from his home with a bundle of hay. He shuffles and strains under its weight, gripping the straps that hold the bundle together. Using his right knee, he thrusts the heavy load forward one step at a time. Next, he hoists the heavy bundle onto one of his concrete walls separating different livestock.

Pulling out a knife, the old man snaps the straps loose, and the hay bundle heaves in relief and expands in a sudden burst. He then spreads the hay across several concrete bays for his cows and donkeys. I can barely see all this over his concrete fence. Mostly, I can see his head, shoulders, and his pitchfork as he sorts the hay.

Throughout the village, within my line of sight, I notice people outside their homes, busy with the tasks of the morning. Each individual moves in syncopation to generate a collective choreography in three-dimensional space.

This all happens atop architecture and in narrow, vertical village walkways, so foreign to me. The mountainous backdrop adds to it all an element of the surreal. As a whole, it is extraordinary. The entire, beautiful spectacle moves about like a musical set, live on stage.

Padma and Dorje say a few words to our hosts, likely discussing itinerary and meals, and then exit the gate to join us in the icy pathway. We begin our day's work.

A golden touch of sunlight highlights the striking dimensions and depth of each surrounding mountain range. A veil has been pulled back, and the true weight and extent of space we now inhabit opens before us. We are ants in a never-ending canyon wilderness.

I remember the oppressive freeze earlier this morning and acknowledge my gratitude for sunlight now on my face, even if the temperature remains unchanged. I wiggle my fingers inside their gloves and do the same with my toes. We embark in the direction of a ridgeline spotted earlier this morning.

As we head up a steep bank at the edge of the last home in the village, I move closer to Radmir and occasionally whisper an observation or two, something new that seems impossible as now part of our new reality in the Himalayas.

He notices the contours of the paths that lead up in many directions from the village and into the heights above. Until now, we had not separated enough from the village to see things like this. *'These must be the paths for typical travel and for prayer shrines along the peaks above.'* I imagine joining a prayer journey on an early morning with a small gathering of monks.

Every new sensory experience adds to the mystique of our "there" moments. I notice a litany of sensory delights: a cow alone, grazing at about 4,500 meters, scrounging for any blade of green poking through the snowy canopy; a lone villager coming home from an overnight trek in God-forsaken temperatures; a Buddhist monk descending from a cliffside prayer shrine.

'Is this real? Is this their 'there?' I wonder silently. *'Or is my snapshot-view tourism distorting reality, creating unnecessary stereotypes? Why is it so difficult to discover authenticity? Even within one's own culture and home, you'd think you know someone only to find out they're a criminal, someone with a heroic past, a secret multi-millionaire, or they're cheating on you. People aren't who you think they are. When a visit like mine is so short, what misconceptions do I create, deceiving myself into thinking I've accessed and understood the real thing about Ladakhi culture?'*

If I allow it, I will lose myself today in my thoughts. I need to stay grounded. I need to remain alert to help search for the gray ghost. *'There will be time to let these thoughts consume me later.'*

Despite my sabotaging mind, I feel the presence of this place. It feels reverent, holy, and so foreign to my own childhood experiences. Growing up, I experienced plenty of the sacred and the religious, but nothing like this.

Radmir and my hushed chatters now cease. The trek takes a more rigorous turn, and we preserve our breath. We walk in silence, taking in everything we are capable of absorbing.

My eyes bound about, as do Radmir's. To save us from snow blindness, we wear sunglasses. Radmir's are Oakley. Mine are a cheap pair I once purchased in Dubai. Everything I see is shades darker than reality behind these lenses. *'Choosing a lens should be a higher priority for me.* **Whatever lens you choose colors the world you see.**'

In this sacred space, there are no billboards or screaming traffic. No foot pedestrians or rattling trains. No rapid subways or multi-colored trash blowing across the ground. No steam from manhole covers or flashing lights from storefront window advertising. No noisy, nosy neighbors. No garbage truck disturbances. No dogs barking. No horns blasting. No arguments in the streets. No streets. Nothing. Only the four of us in the silence of the Himalayan mountainsides and a blanket of bright, bleached snow splashed across the terrain. Just fresh, pure oxygen, albeit in smaller doses than I am used to consuming.

The subtle grandiosity of this entire stage overwhelms and consumes me. I feel enraptured, forgetting that I am here to find the snow leopard. Somehow, the present moment overshadows the entire purpose of the trip; I am enchanted in the here and now.

This is, indeed, one of those "there" places. I know this because in my life, I am all too often thinking about the "next" and the "after," ever planning and preparing. However, my position on this hill has sucked all of the mindless babble of proactive and reactive thinking out of me. It has stripped me down to the bare "now."

I see the indigo sky taking over the remaining, puffy clouds. I hear the crunch of each step on the frozen ground. This menacing cold threatens my entire body. From the last home in the village directly below us, I smell a trailing breakfast fire smoke. *'How special is this place? How am I here? I have become a protagonist in my own journey. This is impossibly beautiful.'*

The cold continues to bite at my toes. *'I put three socks on; I wonder if I should have kept it to two? Maybe I've pressed my feet too tightly against my shoes without room for blood circulation.'* The realization is too late; my feet are already completely numb. *'This is my first novice lesson—take care of my feet,'* I mutter under my breath.

The whole day will probably be painful, each step offering knives of darting agony and the sensation of incessantly buzzing feet. All day will be a class in session, and I will be the student learning my lessons.

Or I can stop, sit dangerously on this ledge, and remove my gloves so that I can proceed to remove my shoes and one layer of socks. This option seems far too risky. I will either make an adjustment at lunch or begin tomorrow.

Knowing there is little I can do now, I resolve to face the situation and glean what I can from it all. '*Who has time to think about pain? There is a snow leopard to see.*' I reassure myself that perseverance will pay off. After enough time in this deadly terrain, the snow leopard will make itself visible to us, eventually.

Hope is my fuel. I press on in the quiet of our expedition. Dorje moves steadily behind us all, and Padma continues to set the pace about fifteen meters ahead. From time to time, she glances back to check on us. If she is smiling, we cannot see it behind her balaclava. However, I am confident she is smiling.

Dorje trots along smoothly, occasionally picking up a rock to inspect it or stooping down to investigate a plant. '*How can he be watching for a snow leopard far in the distance while spotting interesting things at his feet? How is it possible to look far ahead and right in front of you at the same time? How can you entertain a vision for your future and simultaneously notice your family?*

I turn my attention to his gait. As if this were a casual stroll on a beach, he seems in full control of his breathing and fully relaxed. Nothing feels labored or forced.

This reminds me of my own breathing. '*Steady. Slowly. In deep, hold it, count three slow seconds, and now release gradually. Repeat.*' When my mind wanders too far, I find myself out of breath, and I lose my concentration. A little wandering is fine, but it has to be kept in check.

You have to keep the rhythm in this place. I can already see my next lesson manifesting. '*Meditation is not a luxury; it is a necessity. You have to get into a clear state of mind and be fully present. If you fail to do this, you may pass out from lack of oxygen, find yourself disoriented, or fall off the cliff ledge. Patience, calm, rhythm, and attention.*' Repeating these things helps me remember my focus for the day.

As I move to a steadier rhythm while we walk, I notice the musicality, the percussion, of it all. Deep breath, step, step, deep breath, repeat; the crunch of the ice under our feet adds a textured beat. Exhale, step, step, inhale, step, step. Everything moves in my head as a one-beat, followed by a two-beat pattern. *'Heaven's rhythm apparently.'*

Padma continues to pace us, climbing ever higher and higher along this ridge. I have no idea where we are going; I am along for the ride. Once again, I notice the pull of my camera. I concoct a plan to hook the collar gimbal clip into one of my outer jacket layers to relieve some of the strain. It rests comfortably and provides relief, but the weight itself has the same effect on my body. I elect to stick with this plan, as at least my hands are free.

For some time, we weave between ridgeline walks, sheer drop-offs on both sides of the skinny ledge, to then meander down into the valley below and cross over to a new ridgeline. Every few minutes, we pause and scope the horizon lines for any signs.

In each deep valley, a bright, white snake of frozen water cuts through, a reminder of running streams and lush greens in warmer seasons of the year. These icy runs sometimes prove impassable or extremely challenging to traverse if the attempt to pass is made in the wrong place.

Dorje tosses scree all about to act as a grip for our boots on the extremely slick ice. *'Local wisdom.'* I know black ice, but this is a whole other level of slippery. Something about the layers upon layers that have melted and refrozen over time, along with the current temperature conditions, makes this a slick substance unlike anything I have experienced.

It feels like a comedy sketch just trying to scamper across as I slip and flail my way, ever so slowly. Sometimes, the shuffle across the river takes thirty knee-shaking minutes and a few harrowing slips. One moment of lost footing, and I will find myself about one kilometer away from my team and about five hundred meters deeper, down the valley.

As we near and pass over each of these spots along the river, one element impedes our progress: the sun. Sunlight flashes off the frozen river, splashing blinding sparkles in our eyes. Sunglasses help, but the sunlight hampers our progress at times, regardless.

 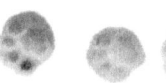

Just before lunch, we happen across a partial blue sheep skeleton as we make our way up into a new searching area. The in-tact horns and bared spine curve into the frozen river, stuck solid. *'What an unforgiving place.'*

This Himalayan desert is one part art, one part death. While this skeleton tells a troubling tale, it also taunts us, teasing us with the reality of a recent snow leopard appearance. *'Its paws graced where our steel-toed boots now grip the ground.'*

After a brief pause in this space, we take another upward trek toward the heavens. With every meter further into the sky, my breath shortens and shallows, and the weight of my legs, bag, and camera weighs heavier on my mind.

A dull ache occupies my lower left flank on my back. Sharp pangs of pain grip my right arm, likely from fatigue. My knee feels unsteady with each step, possibly warning me of meniscus problems in the coming days.

Pain is my reality. However, with a snow leopard on our minds and its presence near us, we have no room for deterrents. We press on.

The pattern now settles into about every fifteen minutes, stopping and scoping the surrounding gullies and horizon lines, in vain attempts to spot the fully camouflaged enigma.

Our guides point in opposite angles in silence. Radmir and I point in equally opposing directions with our cameras, now completing a full compass canvassing the entire terrain.

Not a sound. I feel like Padma and Dorje find things I will never notice. *'They are probably processing all kinds of information from the past and present as they search. They know routes, typical kill sites, see pikas and foxes, but don't need to tell us. They probably see scratch marks and other markers indicating snow leopard.'*

Their training and expertise provide them with the ability to see, understand, interpret, and extrapolate from all of this a strategic plan, a deep understanding. Every plant and animal provides clues in their investigation. Radmir and I see the same things, but search in ignorance, not sure what one clue means versus another. We might as well be blind.

My self-realization is that I am likely more of a hindrance than a help out here. I fail to see as they see, despite continuing to pretend to help, raising the lens viewfinder to my eye, scanning across the tundra.

We are at such an elevation and so deep into the mountains at this point that the auditory absences grow stronger. Only the near-imperceptible breathing can be heard from each of us.

The snap of the cold deadens any sounds. Each step higher isolates us from any noise pollution, even from the rare animal. We climb further and further, pushing ourselves to exhaustion. Inside my boots, I feel my feet rubbing, ripping fresh blister wounds. *'That's a terrible sign. Tonight, foot care will take the number one priority.'*

As for our actual elevation, I have no idea because I did not bring an altimeter. Hypothermia and frostbite are real threats if I dare take off a glove and check the altimeter app on my phone.

I figure concerns about elevation are secondary to searching for the snow leopard; that, any time wasted on checking numbers, distracts my eyes from the prize. If we see one, we see it, no matter the elevation. Another jabbing pain, in my shoulder this time, re-centers me on the narrow path.

Our entire day continues up and back down, rinse and repeat for hours. At this elevation and at these early stages of the trip, these upward scrambles and steep declines take everything out of me. The rocks are unstable, and the snow gives way underneath you all the time.

All this is intensified by the sheer, five-hundred-meter-drop-off ledge to be traversed to reach each new viewpoint. Continuously, my feet rub rawer and rawer. My knees rattle. My fingers ache and tremor under the two layers of gloves, and my balaclava is now wet with my breath's moisture.

Death lurks below at any moment, at any misstep. *'Focus, concentrate; keep pushing; stay determined and hungry; keep meditating; stay in your rhythm; let your senses appreciate everything.'*

These new phrases go on repeat, and I imagine they will be my official mantras for the duration of the trip. The temperatures help numb some pains, but the mental space is the most important in overcoming my physical plight.

Padma continues to pace us. I peek upward toward her location. Mother Nature looks down from above, ready to pounce with a new blanket of snow and a few degrees lower on the death-inviting frigidity scale. We continue into the heavens.

Padma glances back at us and flashes a "thumbs up" sign. I look back, and Dorje signals back to her. *'This whole time I thought they were signaling to Radmir and me.'* I chuckle audibly. *'They were simply communicating with each other.'*

Sometimes, as I walk, a pebble or two falls to the side of the trail. My eyes trace its path downward, hearing each strike against a series of rocks, growing in intensity and speed, echoing its collision cracks off the opposing side's cliffs until its inevitable end in the valley below.

When the ricochets from this commotion diminish and when the simultaneous ricochets of fear in my head subside, I steady my nerves and resume my trek straight up the steep, thin, icy ridgeline.

I remind myself to find my rhythm again. It can be so easy to lose it and all too real when you do. I once again align my steps with my breaths in that two-one pattern. *'This is like meditation training on steroids; if I was ever ambivalent before, I'm certain of its medicinal power now.'* Too fatigued to navigate this tricky terrain, I have to engage in a meditative state or proceed at my own peril.

A few steps later, and I am lost in my mind again. This time, I travel deeper into a daydream. Suddenly, I am transported to an earlier time in life.

"'How do you do it,? I mean, all this crap. Where do you find the time?" My college study partner holds his hands out in disbelief, a blank but sincere stare blanketed across his face.

"I don't know. I just make sure each hour is accounted for, I guess." I answer with agitation because we have to keep working on the presentation, but he keeps insisting on side chatter. My fingers tap the table.

"You just constantly do things. What drives you?"'

In this instant, my foot slips on an ice-covered rock, and I tumble to the ground, sliding down the side of the cliff edge. Whipping my hand in a violent jerk, I dig my gloved fingers into the edge of a large boulder. This rapid reaction staves off a complete, perilous fall.

I lay there panting for a few seconds. My crisis has been averted, but the fall has hurt my right knee. Possibly, it is only a bruise on my patella. The attempt to stabilize my fall exhausted me of my physical stamina; I allow each limb to lie limp on the steep incline. Besides, more surface area helps keep me pinned to the steep ledge.

I am reminded of my camera. With much laboring, I lift it and check for scuffs or scrapes; everything looks good. There is only a small scratch on the lens body. Again, crisis averted. At least I can still see things through my camera lens.

With a very slow and deliberate pivot, I rotate onto my stomach so that I can army-crawl back up to the path. I start pushing upward across loose scree on a near-vertical plane until I near the original path where I fell.

By now, Radmir, Padma, and Dorje stand a meter above me. Their eyes bulge wide, and panic colors their shouts. I can see their rapid movements, but their words sound muffled. 'Have I damaged my ears? I can't make out what they're saying, even though they are mere meters away. '*Are they even shouting? Or is every sound exaggerated?*

After seeing my brief fall, they must have hurried to my place on the path. As I edge even closer and within reach, Dorje extends his tripod to my left-hand side, and Padma extends hers to my right. Together, they pull me back to my feet.

 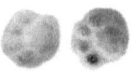   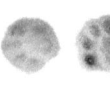

I still myself and regain a slowed pattern of breathing while Radmir holds me up. *'That's the last time I'll let my mind wander. That could have been it right there.'* I must have half-deliriously uttered these words audibly.

Radmir leans down and whispers to me, "What did you say?"

"Oh. Sorry," I pant between each word until I muster momentum for the remainder of the sentence and rattle it off quickly. "Just mumbling to myself about how stupid-dangerous that fall was," I whisper back.

"More careful. You must. Please," pleads Padma. "Every step you must carefully watch and not fall." I know I have lost some of their trust. This will be difficult to regain in such taxing circumstances.

"I know, I know," I whisper between still-heavy breaths.

"Should I let you down to sit for a bit?" Radmir asks.

"Sure, yeah. Let me." I lose the sentence to a need for breath. "Phew. Um. Okay." My chest-heaving exhales grow in intensity. "For a minute." I slump to the icy path and rest. Any talking burdens me further.

They, all three, stand around me with frowns and concerned stares. After a few minutes, my breath comes back, and my adrenaline levels lower. I take a few sips of water and gather some strength. As Padma and Radmir lift me back to my feet, I stand and then bend over, hands clutching my knees for support. I concentrate on slow, deliberate breaths.

Dorje pulls his scope out, in the meantime, and looks at some places along the valley floor once he sees I am improving and upright again. After a few more minutes, I feel strong enough to continue. The pain in my knee has subsided, and I feel like the fright of the fall was greater than the reality of it all.

Dorje collects his gear and begins slowly back up the trail again, asking us to follow. Now Padma will take the rear.

"Josh is okay. Just a little fall," whispers Padma as Dorje walks past. Everyone nods and sees that I have composed myself from this fall.

I tamp the ground a couple of times to get the snow off my pants, and I steady my footing by kicking in a foothold into the frozen path. Sucking in a couple of deep breaths, I get back into the mental state needed to trek upward once again. In the face of fear and weakness, I step forward.

This time, I am fully locked into a meditative state with a renewed commitment to avoid any mental wanderings. My mind centers on every step, and every muscle pulls taut with stabilizing intensity.

Every time the mind attempts to wander, I drag it back, kicking and screaming, to the current moment on this sheer cliff side, within possible eyesight of the snow leopard. *'I bet any leopard watching us right now got a good laugh out of that fall. How futile our attempts to go to the heavens and visit the gray ghost. I am a fool to try this. And I'm so happy I am.'*

Radmir pats me on the back and flashes an encouraging smile underneath his balaclava. This team is impressive. Here alone in nature, the few of us together are quite strong. I may be the weakest link, but if that is true, we are a formidable force. *'Mother Nature has her work cut out for her.'*

I listen to the crackling snow, ice, and rock beneath me, regaining my two-one pattern. My awareness of the swish-swish of my pant legs rubbing against each other adds a layer of rhythm to my steps that I had not noticed before. Swoosh, crunch, swoosh, crunch, breath; swoosh, crunch, swoosh, crunch, exhale. Repeat.

Now that I pay closer attention, I notice another sound. My backpack rubs against my goose down summit jacket, adding a wisping flutter every time it shifts from left to right. Each step causes the backpack to change position slightly on my back.

This extra soft swoosh combines with my footsteps, pant legs, and breath to create an intoxicating orchestral performance. Out here in this remote Himalayan plane, it might as well be the world's most prolific, accidental ensemble.

I tune in further, beyond the auditory. I see a whiteout, snowy expanse interrupted by occasional birds, both small and large. Massive boulders crowd in the sun-splashed river frozen below. These gigantic rocks boast

mostly gray and orange hues, the same hues we saw coming up here from Leh. I feel the last roll of a sweat bead round the lip and touch the tongue; a tangy, salty tinge tickles my taste receptors once again.

Yes, even in the cold, due to all those layers and our level of intensity trekking, there is salt because there is sweat, and it drips occasionally from underneath my hat and balaclava.

Now my foot pain moves from raw rubbing to a jabbing, persistent prick. My fingers no longer tremor, but tingle. The weight of my camera and lens pulls me to the ground, stronger with each step. *'With all this effort, we have to see something. Where are you, dear snow leopard?'*

Suddenly, the mind wanders again—to work, to relationships, to conversations from my younger years.

"What do you mean I have to start over again?"

"You didn't pass the driver's exam. That's it."

"But I only missed this one—

"I said, you failed, and that's it. Try better next time. You can reschedule in the office over there." I can see my father's empathetic eye as I approach him, head down.

~~~

"Don't put that on that way. Don't you know how to solder a coupling? It's a coupling. You like being an apprentice, do you? Because you keep making stupid mistakes like this, you'll always be an apprentice, a nothing. You put the solder tip like this and don't overheat the fitting."

I sit there in apathetic rebellion. Under my breath, I mutter something along the lines of not giving a crap and that I'm in college anyway and have another career path and you can just go to hell with your abusive garbage.

~~~

"Oh my God. She's beyond beautiful. How have I not seen someone this beautiful until now?"

"She's outta your league, dude. Don't even think about making a fool of yourself."

"You're right." I resign to sit this adventure out. There's no way I can get this girl. Not with this limited time in Mexico. Not with everyone else watching. Who am I fooling? I wouldn't get her attention even if I tried.

~~~

"Take the shot. Take the goddam shot. Josh! Take it." Coach's face is blood-red, and the veins bulge heavily against his pit-stained white collared shirt as he races along the sideline. Spittle splatters on the court. 'He's gonna blow a gasket this time.'

The crowd screams incessantly. I know I'm in over my head. I'm too timid, too shy, too scared of the moment.

Swirling around the defender, I angle toward the basket. Two defenders crouch in on me, and I shovel a pass out to the perimeter. Aaron takes the shot and misses.

"C'mon, Josh! You gotta take that shot! Damnit!"

~~~

"I'm afraid the ankle is so bad that there's no point worrying about further damage by forcing the swelling out. It's been a month. We have to reduce this swelling to obtain better images and see the extent of the damage to your peroneal medial and lateral tendons.

So, Mom and Dad, can you come to either side of him and get a good grip? Son, bite down on this towel and keep your tongue back in your mouth. We'll give you morphine right after this."

My fingers dig into the medical table, piercing through the thin, light brown covering. The swift twist and subsequent crack still haunt me today.

That night, with my leg elevated on the backrest of the couch, I wondered how many more months I would suffer, unable to do anything during my best years of high school.

~~~

Shaking my head perceptibly, I force myself to snap back to the present. My thoughts seem to whirl at a more rapid pace now, jumping from one point in time to another. *'Why can't I imagine being "here" at the homestay and in these Himalayas? Why does my mind keep wandering?'*

My foot skids, but I catch myself this time. The reaction time is more precise. I am more attuned to imminent danger. *'No one noticed that one; we're good. Keep going. Keep pressing on. Show Dorje, Padma, and Radmir you're made out for this. There's a snow leopard date at the end of this trial.'*

I glance over at Radmir. *'How's he holding up? He seems good.'* He keeps a good pace and remains steady on the path. He is short of breath, but that seems to be his only physical restriction.

The sun persists brightly above. Snow trickles down from time to time from some random cloud gathering, but it seems most of the snow falls in the night. As we enter into the early afternoon, the whole purpose of this venture—the gray ghost—takes a back seat to our constant encounters.

Fascinating rock formations, a few small mammals, large birds of prey overhead, and continual deafening silence all hold our attention. I am so immersed in everything, at least when I am not lost in my own thoughts. This entire place is hauntingly barren and immensely rich simultaneously.

Right before lunch, we stop and rest for a short while. I pull out a cheap scope I brought along with me to give it a try—a Celestron Ultima 80. It proves difficult to stabilize with my unsteady hands.

I also brought along a cheap tripod to hold the scope, but it bends under the weight. Attempting to stabilize the tripod, I grab some large rocks and strategically place them around each of the legs. I stack them about three rocks high. Even then, a slight breeze causes minor sways that disturb any practical use for the scope.

Soon enough, I give up, disconnect the scope from the feeble tripod, and lie back on the ground. Using my knees to stabilize the scope, I give it another try. Unfortunately, even this attempt fails to make this scope useful. My neck strains, and my core tires out within minutes. *'This is a waste of time. This scope isn't equipped for these distances, visual distortions, or cold. Either that, or it is user error, and I just don't get it.'*

I return to my heavy friend. Despite its beefy composition, I find my camera setup to be more effective for searching. I lug the burden of fifteen pounds back out and bring the viewfinder to my eye. My muscles strain to hold things in place. *'I'll see something if it's the last thing I do.'*

Our guides diligently search the north and south. Both Padma and Dorje take off their outermost, upper layers as the sun has provided some semblance of warmth. They wear camouflage thermals as their middle layer. *'That's dedication, to know that you may still need camo after you de-layer.'* I cannot imagine taking any layers off, even at this point. The weather might still freeze you in place, no matter the presence of the sun. *'Pure insanity. You would have to be from here to remove layers and still thrive in these temperatures.'*

They have liner gloves like Radmir and me, and a summit glove on the outside. As it is midday now, they have removed their outer gloves. *'What are they? Superhuman? I won't be removing my gloves at any point today.'*

Dorje and Padma rub their hands synchronously together and perform occasional standing leg curls while they scope to keep the blood moving.

These motions become a sort of ritual. I imagine they have conducted these movements a myriad times before on these lonely peaks. The simplicity and alignment of their actions together create an intoxicating rhythm, yet another percussion and pattern to appreciate.

Meanwhile, I set my camera down for a few minutes to mimic their behavior and then do about twelve pushups. Blood movement and warmth return to me. *'Always study and follow the actions of those who know how to live here,'* I remind myself.

At last, Padma finds a spot for lunch. It is quite late in the afternoon. *'Maybe they needed to really get a sense of snow leopard activity before we stopped to eat on this first day.'*

We settle in next to a prominent stupa, a Buddhist shrine. Impressive stupas are scattered across this region. We have spotted a few outside the village and higher up in the hills. *'Is there any place better to meditate on the divine than here?'*

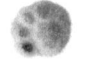 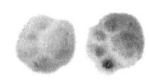

I glance at Radmir, and he shakes his head in disbelief. "How are we at this insane elevation next to a gorgeous stupa, having lunch after looking for snow leopards for half a day?" He says all this with a smile, with hand gestures that sway left and right to account for the entire scene. As he speaks, I can see my reflection in his sunglasses. I look small.

I glance over at the stupa. Outside of a few other mountain peaks in the death zone, which are not habitable anyway, these stupas represent man's closest approach to connect with God, to reach out and touch the heavens. *'This is the closest to God we mortals can reach with feet still planted on earth.'* No wonder they pray here.

Another "there" to feel and see for myself, a "there" that transcends words. *'No doubt, I've flown over this spot at some point and wish I could be down here exploring this "there." Here I am. Someday, no matter my religious persuasion, I must return to one of these stupas and attempt to communicate with the divine and do it in silence for at least a few weeks.'*

Padma and Dorje operate like machines. In hushed quiet, they each assume their roles and go about preparing lunch seamlessly. One bends to gather bread while another bends the other way to gather condiments. Back and forth, they ebb and flow in harmony until the job is complete. In minutes, an impressive spread lies before us.

We scarf down chicken sandwiches, chocolate chip cookies, and boxed mango juice. Everything tastes simple and perfect. They treat us like kings in a kingdom we do not deserve.

By now, I have lost the will to change the layers in my socks. Besides, the slight warmth of midday has made it bearable for my feet. *'But tomorrow, I have to make some changes to my clothing and gear arrangements,'* I promise myself.

Soon enough, we rise and continue. Padma and Dorje pack up with the same precision and efficiency as the setup. Padma approaches us and says, "It is time. We go." She smiles and waves her arm at us as if to invite us to the next level of a video game.

Lunch provided a sort of return to normalcy. Sitting down and eating a meal is an everyday experience. It pulled me back into the commonplace ever so slightly. Padma's sudden call to move again, along with our eyes looking skyward toward our path, reminds me that this experience is nothing ordinary.

'*Am I really here? Searching for snow leopards? In the Himalayas?*'

Dorje sets out and establishes the pace this time, with Padma taking the rear. We head back onto the path and charge deeper into the mountainous wilderness.

I remind myself about our loneliness out here. I remind myself that being here at this time of year ensures solitude, which I appreciate, but adds difficulty to our quest. I remind myself that the lack of additional eyes, scopes, and foot power from the large groups of tourists during mating season is our reality.

We will have to see everything ourselves. The responsibility to scour each valley and ridge is up to us and us alone.

We are a four-person team, working like horses, and any success will depend on our stamina, determination, mindset, eyes, and legs. This task will push our bodies to their utter limits, and this realization steels my will.

Again, silence consumes us as we travel higher. Like an old friend, the auditorily vacant space revisits us and keeps us company with each new precarious step. Our elevation is so immense that our place in relation to the clouds is unclear: one minute, we might stand high above the clouds, while the next minute, we stand surrounded by a heavy, snowing blanket of thickness. Thankfully, the majority of this first day has been in the sun with only light cloud cover.

We search in vain. It seems like hours since lunch, but it has probably only been thirty minutes. My sense of time and place is jumbled, and I am too exhausted to check my phone for the time. As far as I can tell, we have discovered no promising signs that might indicate a snow leopard in our midst.

More crow caws and more steep steps continue to be our reality, scree underneath our feet giving way and tumbling down the cliff to our sides.

 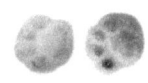

At this point, the sun rests below the highest peaks in the western distance. Shadows begin to creep across the canyons, the opposite of the morning's spectacle. The beginning of dusk has arrived. Like a parent shutting off the lights for bedtime, Mother Nature warns us that her natural light wanes, and it is time to go home and find safety.

The return of deathly chill fills the air and pains the lungs. The sunshine had provided some abatement to the fierceness of the cold. Now, unimpeded, the cold grips me tightly and rattles me to the core.

I glance over at Radmir, and I see the desperation for warmth in his eyes as his lashes begin to frost above his balaclava. Just thinking about how many hours we have left to reach the homestay creates a physical shiver from head to toe.

Padma and Dorje both suggest we initiate our return for dinner. "Shall we go now? Time for dinner; we will eat at the homestay," Dorje whispers with an orange-blue sky dancing menacingly behind him.

Fatigued beyond words, I vaguely realize we have all agreed to begin the return trek to the homestay. They turn around and shuffle forward, and I follow suit, more mechanically than anything else.

My senses have been badgered, bewildered, and overwhelmed. They have no more capacity to absorb. I walk numbly. As we make our way, I try to stay conscious enough to maintain my breathing rhythm and focus on my foot placement. Before long, my mind wanders, and I reflect on the day.

All in all, this first day greeted us with a few blue sheep far into the distance, a couple of chirping pikas, several Asian golden eagles soaring high overhead, a constant group of crows following us, and the occasional local resident traveling between villages.

No snow leopard. The ghost slips our grasp today. However, there is tomorrow, and it offers the promise of possibility.

Despite the difficult physical reality of today, beauty is what I remember most. 'Yes, I think today can be summarized as terribly beautiful.' Reflection grows stronger as the homestay comes into view. 'How many hours have we *walked back to the homestay?'* Again, the sense of time is completely lost on me.

Darkness now prevails, and we continue with the aid of the moon's brilliance. The moon reflecting off the snow generates enough light such that we do not need our head torches.

Before I know it, we pass through the gated entrance to our haven. Palden and Dahla place before us hot steaming carrot soup, sticky rice, fresh beef, and gooey bread. The reward for the day's toils goes down smoothly and warms every part of me.

The center of the room glows from the freshly lit fire. It serves well to save us from our shaking, painfully wintry disposition. Padma and Dorje finally join us now that they have packed away their gear. We sit on cushions on the floor, gulping down dinner. No one talks; we eat in silence.

After some time, the warmth of the fire and food has brightened our hearts and cleared our heads. I feel like I can once again see everything around me and enjoy the company of others. Eventually, conversations begin among us. Padma once again shares stories of previous tourist visits and their successes.

Candlelight fills the room and sparkles in her eyes. Her stories match this sparkle and come alive with hope and possibility. She tells us of the Norwegian team earlier in the year, in March, when they had five sightings. And there was an Indian group and a surprising seven total sightings.

Then there was the time the snow leopard walked right through their village, mere meters from the Ladakhi families out and about their homes that fateful evening in February. Everyone was safe despite the close encounter. Village homes buzzed in conversation about its ghostly visitor.

Then there was the Canadian group, who had two sightings, but one very close with a kill in a ravine. There was another group, which was made up of mixed nationalities, who saw three snow leopards. All of these have occurred within the past year.

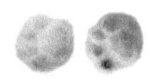

The tales encourage us. We swallow these stories just as we swallowed dinner, and they nourish us. We hang on Padma's every word. Both stomach and mind bask in the beauty and rest of the moment.

"Nature never says when or where, you know. You must be ready. You must be strong all the time. Challenges come, and you push into the mountain very far. And as we go, we carry much respect and love with us. Protect people and snow leopard, this is what we do. Live together in harmony."

Padma speaks with a sincerity in her tone and body language. Her pace is deliberate and calculated. She holds these words like heirloom diamonds handed down through the years. Her wisdom shines brightly.

Dorje stares straight ahead. He is somewhere else in his mind. Perhaps recalling the tales his father and mother would have told him. As Padma finishes her thoughts, he chimes in: "You know, we haven't always had good relations with snow leopard. We learn over a long time. We find a better way to live together. Snow leopard no longer hurts our animals because we have better protection; also, we learn not to hurt the leopard. It is because we understand more. It is also our belief in Nirodha. We suffered, all of us, for a long time. Now, we understand, and we protect each other. We live for each other, man and the ghost." In between each statement, he would pause in seeming reflection, similar to Padma.

After back-to-back nights of dinner tales, I feel relieved that I have come to know a bit more about Dorje and Padma. Inconspicuously, I peel back my Columbia sweater to sneak a glance at the edge of my Eternal Knot tattoo. *'Interconnectedness. Wisdom. Balance.'*

Dahla and Palden listen silently as they rest on the far end of the room. *'I can't even imagine what they think, believe, or feel about all this. About tourist invaders into their home. About the lore, beauty, and nuisance the leopard has been for them over the decades.'*

I recall an interview I conducted with Dr. Tsewang Namgail, the director of the Snow Leopard Conservancy India Trust, some years before. I remember the many projects his team had initiated to create peace between the snow leopard and the human communities connected with the cat.

They finally found a way to protect their livestock from the leopards, and this created harmony. They use solar sound alarms that keep the snow leopards away. They build safer, fully enclosed pens for their livestock, which proved far more effective than their previous designs. The community attends regular training sessions about the gray ghost and about peaceful cohabitation strategies.

All this, along with the money they get from tourists, has helped build a more positive relationship with the snow leopard. *'But what do they really think and feel about all the change?'* Palden and Dahla's faces remain stoic, devoid of any emotions.

While my mind wanders, Dorje's words roll off his tongue and place the entire room into a trance-like state. Radmir and I learn; we try to understand. We attempt to see.

Padma adds more to the conversation. She speaks of the myths of Kinnara and Kinnari. As she shares, we learn of these beings who will guide us and watch over us in this expedition.

They will show us the way. At this point in the night, I start to lose my stamina. *'This is just too much to take in for one day. This is the "there" I always seek. But it can be too much to take in when taken in such large quantities or in the extreme. I feel like today has been a firehose into the Ladakhi and Himalayan trekking and cultural experience.'*

Everything fills me to the brim until it spills over and out onto the floor. My mind scrambles to capture as much as possible and mitigate loss. This is heaven.

Ultimately, this first day consisted of twelve hours of intense trekking and meditation, along with a dangerous fall. Becoming one with nature proved beyond cliché in this spiritual space.

I found that becoming "one with nature" requires a departure from the natural into a more spiritual, meditative state. You have no other choice but to embrace spirituality, as nothing feels like the "natural" you are familiar with experiencing. Besides, as I see it, today I learned that one must become one with Mother Nature or become a victim of her treachery. She demands this level of respect.

 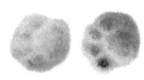   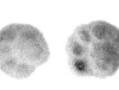

Tonight, after I tend to the sores on my feet, I fall asleep immediately, unaware of anything other than my body's aching for rest. Radmir and I do not even bother with a fire in our room. We simply dash to our respective beds, curl under the blankets, and pass out.

Too beaten down from the day's labor, I fall asleep, completely unaware and having forgotten about the dark presence in the room earlier that morning.

Before I realize it, our alarms sound off in the dark morning of the next day. Today repeats much like the first, with no promise of snow leopards.

It starts with an embrace of the morning's piercing chill, before the sun wakes up. Today offers a different set of valleys and ridgelines. We see a few more blue sheep, and closer to us this time. We find the scat of a Tibetan wolf; this was super exciting. However, the repetition continues in the forms of walking, meditation, aching cold, absence of sound, and the absence of the gray ghost.

I feel stronger today, and Radmir seems stronger as well. We keep up easily with our guides, and every corner is another wonderland of surprises with jagged edges, cliffs, and glistening ice. We end the night in tales over dinner just as the day before, bellies and hearts full.

Dinner is fresh, steaming yak stew, warm bread, hot milk tea, and creamy potatoes. Dorje leads the storytelling. After a day of trekking and a night warm with tales, we go to bed physically spent but so blessed to be in this hallowed space with these incredible people.

Radmir and I settle into our beds quickly tonight; we are keenly aware of each day's physical toils and the necessity for sleep. As such, we have found our routine already on day two: bathroom visits, quick packing for the next morning, placement of items under our blankets for safekeeping in the cold, and then we throw ourselves under the blankets in our respective beds.

Tonight, I am more aware of my surroundings because I am getting used to the physical demands of the day. I have an increased capacity. As a result, instead of immediately falling asleep, I rest in the darkness, thinking and looking around.

And then it happens. I notice it again. Creeping along the walls is the darkness. It seems to have extended now across the entire ceiling beyond its initial containment to the corner, with some parts stretched even further out onto the ceiling. It pulsates and gags, more pronounced than before.

My eyes widen, my heart lurches, and my tongue sticks to the roof of a suddenly dry mouth. Awkwardly, I gasp, sucking in a squeal of air. Fingertips claw into the first layer of blankets and squeeze. *'What on earth?' Is it actually real? I can't be hallucinating a second time.'* With the visage of this ghastly entity now clearly before me, undeniably real, my chest tightens, and my forearms and biceps squeeze.

I stare at it in the night's darkness. It is just murky enough in here to retain some disbelief. In this instant, my mind attempts to argue against what the eyes see. Likely, my mind has filled in the gaps of what is unseen with wild, grotesque images of this pulsating, tentacled being, sprawled out on the wall and ceiling.

I cast doubt on the entire image. *'There is no way I'm seeing things right.'* It is just too shadowy to tell for sure. Even if my eyes deceive me, some kind of bad presence prowls in the room. I sense it crawling.

Eventually, I feel light-headed from holding in my breath and silently straining my eyes to see the evil surrounding me in this room. After some time, I must have fallen asleep from sheer exhaustion.

In the morning, the darkness is gone. I convince myself once again that the whole thing is nothing but a figment of my imagination and go about the day's routine. *'Nothing is there, and we have to start searching this morning. I don't have time to think about whatever I keep seeing.'*

On this third day, we go out as usual in the morning to investigate. Some light snow falls while we walk. The clouds grow thick and heavy around us.

After completing our reconnaissance session, breakfast time offers a surprise. Instead of breakfast at our host's home, we visit another homestay and meet new people.

 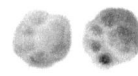

This new home's living room is surprisingly warm, with a heavy dose of sunrays baking in through the clouds, through the latticed windows, and onto the traditional Ladakhi carpets. Radmir and I soak in the heat.

A group of women from the village is already seated inside. With open arms and wide smiles, they invite us over for tea and bread. Within minutes, we begin enjoying the meal set before us; everything tastes exquisite.

We drink butter tea. It is satisfying, made up of yak milk, tea leaves, and salt. The thick, rich flavors consume and warm. Usually, I find tea to be mostly light and watered down with a touch of bitterness. Ladakhi butter tea is different.

After the morning recon mission, this visit is just what the doctor ordered. The community's hospitality and warmth continue to embrace us.

We exit the home after expressing our gratitude and again see the children at play and the adults at work. In a way, this quaint village has a hustle and bustle that rivals any major city.

With newfound energy from the surprise breakfast visit, we make our way back up into the cliffs once again. Radmir and I find ourselves adjusting to the cold nicely now.

We are discovering which clothing items are optimal, which sock arrangements keep the feet the least cold, how to balance weight and necessities in one's daypack, and at what times it is safe to remove our summit gloves, leaving us with just the liner gloves but better dexterity. Experience is the best teacher.

I also find that my footing is more stable and my breathing stronger. I have a better rhythm, and the mind wanderings interrupt me less frequently. The whole experience becomes more immersive, and my meditative state consumes a larger portion of the day than when I first began on day one.

Today, we find semi-fresh snow leopard paw prints and a fresh urine marking about a three-hour walk from the homestay, along a false peak.

In the night, the ghost passed by and marked a large rock. Because the snow in the morning was light, we were still able to make out the paw prints.

Radmir's face glows with excitement. I pull my balaclava back so that I can flash my grin to the team. "This is amazing," I say, studying Dorje's expressions to understand how informative this data is toward a real sighting.

"I need to capture this," says Radmir as he pulls off a glove with his teeth and snaps a few photos. The Coolpix camera is always ready at his side.

"This is good news," suggests Padma. "We cannot know for certain, but maybe it's good. We miss the leopard in the night, but this means the leopard in our area right now and searching for food."

Everything they ever encounter reveals something important. Experience and wisdom continue to combine into a powerful duo for Padma and Dorje. They are masters of their domain.

Dorje says the words we know to be true but tantalize us: "We wait for nature to speak to us, to show us the way."

But what if nature never shows us? What if we aren't listening? What if Radmir and I distract you and Padma from seeing and hearing from nature? These counterarguments run silently as I observe Padma and Dorje's body language. At last, I respond, forcing more hope into my tone to compensate for my frustration with missing this leopard.

"Very good news." I adjust my balaclava back in place and take a few photos as well. Once we collect all the information we can, Padma leads us onward in the general direction of the prints. "Let's go see," she says, stepping back into motion.

What will it mean to see? An actual snow leopard sighting? Just more clues? If we see nothing at all, is that seeing? Already, I feel disappointment and cynicism taking hold of me.

In the face of these rising emotions, I choose to press onward, reminding myself that the journey is important. No one arrives in Leh and sees

 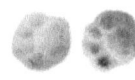

snow leopards, one after another, bounding about the cliffs. This is a slow, laborious, meditative journey.

As the day progresses, we find small groups of blue sheep again, which continues to be promising. In the absence of other snow leopard signs, blue sheep means prey, which means the gray ghost should be lurking around somewhere nearby.

"These sheep are very special to us and to snow leopard. They are the balance of nature, the connection together. The snow leopard needs sheep, and the sheep learn to be strong and survive because of snow leopard," Padma whispers. My tattooed arm quivers under all the layers.

We all stand and watch them interact for a while. The males bash horns in an attempt at maintaining or establishing dominance. With ease, they jump about on sheer cliffs as if they were on level ground. The spectacle mesmerizes. Before we know it, an hour passes.

Later in the day, we see more pikas, eagles, and crows. The terrain continues to prove bitterly Arctic and unforgiving. Another light dusting of snow greets us just before lunch.

On the one hand, this is good for finding fresh tracks. On the other hand, it presents navigation challenges as already-packed snow or ice now has a new, slick layer on top, making difficult trekking even more challenging.

Soon enough, we stop for lunch. Dorje reaches out and hands us our meals. Again, it soothes hunger pangs and energizes us for the afternoon scampers and searches.

After lunch, we repeat the now-familiar process of walking for a while and then anchoring to scope for a short time. The cycle begins to form a hypnotic pattern. I feel myself settling into the rhythm of it all.

Just before the sun descends behind the colosseum of peaks around us, Padma raises her hand. Dorje, Radmir, and I whip our heads in her direction. She stands firm without movement, her right eye socket glued to the scope and her left hand still raised for attention.

Dorje pivots and swings his scope in her direction. They are just close enough to exchange some whispers in Ladakhi. I feel helpless. *'What are they seeing? Is it a snow leopard?*

My heart rate increases rapidly. I feel blood rush throughout my body in excitement. It is the first time I have felt warmth today. Radmir's eyes are wide and intense, bouncing between Dorje and Padma, trying to get a sense of what they see.

After a few minutes, Radmir scoots next to Padma to gather intel. I move over toward Dorje. There is heightened intensity in their gestures. Something is happening, but I cannot tell what it is.

After a few minutes of silence and bated breath, they turn from whispering to low voices. This is our cue that it is not a snow leopard.

'But what is it? What's so important to stop everything and look?'

Dorje points me to the scope and asks me to observe. "I don't know what I'm looking for. What am I seeing?" I ask anxiously. My gloved hands tremble and struggle to hold the scope still.

"It is a Tibetan Wolf. Wolf died after maybe long fall from the peak. We must watch for snow leopard in this area. She may come to eat." Dorje has both dashed and renewed our hopes simultaneously.

A Tibetan Wolf is not the snow leopard, but still an amazing sighting, even though it has passed. This wolf might be food for the snow leopard and, indeed, may attract attention.

Padma looks more closely through the scope and adds disappointing news. "But the wolf is probably frozen. I think no animal comes to eat right now." Just like that, our roller coaster called "hope" takes another nosedive. "After a few months, the wolf will be ready for eating, once the snow is gone," she continues.

This is something I would have never calculated. I would just assume that a dead animal would attract predators. Given that no predator visited the deceased animal while it was fresh, it is now too frozen to be edible.

 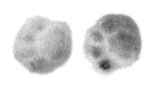

It takes a few minutes, when we resume walking, to come down off the high of the wolf sighting. The adrenaline rushes through the body and takes over. Having felt it a few times now, I have come to expect this interruption as part of the pattern of our meditation. When the adrenaline hits, I feel like an animal, darting my eyes around the landscape with renewed possibilities of seeing something.

We end the day with only the wolf sighting and the promising signs from earlier that morning. Exhaustion, blisters, and numbness define the evening. Emotionally and physically, we are spent.

Thankfully, the pain is short-lived as dinner, prepared by Dahla and Palden, touches our tongues. Pain subsides and is replaced with pleasure. Once again, the meal is their gift of love. While we exchange few words, the sharing of a meal becomes the communal act between our hosts and ourselves.

The next few days repeat just like before; long days in unforgiving freeze and finding very little in the way of the snow leopard except for a few tracks here or there. The signs encourage us, but without actual sightings, everything feels like we are chasing our shadows. Clearly, we chase a ghost.

Discouragement creeps in, and nagging doubt gnaws with every dinner. It grows, slowly, in intensity each night. '*What if there's no chance? What if we planned this trip when it's too cold and there are not enough eyes on the ridgelines, not enough people helping us? What if we're missing every possible sighting because there are too few of us to see what needs to be seen?*'

Of course, all these thoughts prove foolish. The breadth of cultural and human experiences already exceeds expectations. The trip is its own reward regardless of a snow leopard sighting. We have entered an enchanted world and are reveling in every moment.

Even though this is true, sometimes, it is difficult to set the goal aside and appreciate the present moment. Too often, we look over the shoulder of today, jealously flirting with the promise of tomorrow's agenda. Consequently, I feel stuck between gratitude and disappointment. I wish to will myself to love only the journey, but my nature, my shallow need for an achieved goal, still pulls at me.

As we turn to bed each night, the nagging dark presence persists in our room. It creeps from the walls and inches closer to me with each passing night. While all else remains constant, this is the one change I have come to expect. It grows thicker and darker. The pulsing expansion increases in diameter.

It was easier to pass it off as an illusion and something just in my head for the first two days. Tonight, on day six, it has me by the throat. Two long, sticky globs reach down from the ceiling and clutch my neck. The feeling is not violent. Rather, it is like a slow, thick, and heavy puff of tainted air hovering around my face and restricting my mouth.

I feel slightly suffocated as it rests heavily around my face. I breathe, but as if through a straw. *'What is this stuff? How come I can't see it in the day? How does Radmir not see it?'*

For fear of Radmir thinking I am crazy, I have been scared of bringing it to his attention. He has no reaction when I see it in the night. He even glances in its direction but does not show any expression. *'Obviously, he must not see it. Or maybe, like me, he is too frightened to discuss it.'*

He sleeps calmly on the other side of the room, apparently oblivious to this horrible presence I see and feel. After a struggle for some time, I fall asleep, with this presence torturing me.

I know by daylight it will cower back into a corner and disappear; this stiffens my courage to sleep. I know that I will emerge seemingly unscathed by the morning, ready to take on the lofty peaks. I allow it to have its way with me in the night, and know I will be fine in the morning.

On the seventh day, we visit another member of the community before we venture out on yet another grueling day's quest. We walk down the road, past a few homes, to another homestay. Here, women have already gathered early this morning to make stuffed snow leopard, ibex, and sheep figurines.

The women sit scattered about randomly throughout the home. They look picturesque in their placement, like the painting *The Last Supper*. Suddenly, their placement appears less random and more artistic.

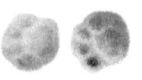

A hazy smoke swirls across the ceiling, evidence of a salivating breakfast or incense burning in a nearby room. Light fragments dance throughout the room through the latticed windows.

In this home, thin, deep maroon curtains help cast a dark red tint to the entire working space. Hovering the room is verbal silence mixed with felt crafting tools in action, their slight sounds of clings, stabs, and rubs. All workers busy themselves in silent dedication.

Each woman crafts using only natural dyes along with sheep and yak wool. Their fingers move in dizzying speeds, whirling and weaving dazzlingly intriguing pieces. I cannot keep track of each hand's movement; every hand blurs in the dim room.

The woman's face nearest me remains statuesque while her hands work, contrastingly, in rapid strokes. Each maneuver of the needle manifests new contours and colors. These incredible women are another manifestation of everything I have come to understand about this village: every act, every single piece of felt wool is a gift of love and precision. *'I would never have put the idea of precision, a mostly clinical word in my mind, with that of love. What an interesting combination.'*

Furthermore, consistent with everything I have seen so far, this work is a way of sharing, a way of helping those outside the Rumbak valley to see and understand. These beautiful people open themselves and share what they have with the world. I see this in Palden and Dahla. It is evident in Dorje and Padma. Furthermore, it emanates from the work of these women.

Because of this communal dedication, their work escapes the normal consumerism approaches found in so many product-creation environments. These creations tell a story of their lives; they tell a story of their origins, survival, and values. These animal figurines offer a window into a uniquely Ladakhi world of reverence mixed with a healthy fear of nature.

Furthermore, this work is not that of mere greed. It is a testament to Ladakhi women's determined quest for freedom and self-sufficiency. The proceeds from these crafts provide a mechanism for the women to hold currency. In Ladakhi history, these women have more spending power and freedom than ever before. They have a greater voice and broader influence in the community.

Being about so much more than cultural expression, these crafts have come to represent equality, resilience, power, persistence, and grace.

The irony causes me to chuckle slightly out loud. *'The ways of antiquity, of traditionally and stereotypically feminine, such as weaving and felting, are now used as tools for women's progress. Who knew the old-fashioned ways had merit? Once again, the wisdom of old proves effective. These women are models for the world to see; they've forged their way against all odds. Their lives, their actions are the testament to this fact.'*

We choose to mainly observe and avoid speaking to the workers this morning because they are busy. From the sales representative in the adjoining room of the house, we purchase a few items and then rejoin Padma and Dorje outside.

After this brief visit, we embark on yet another day in paradise, close to the heavens, in search of the gray ghost, and in full physical self-destruction mode. *'Let the punishment of Mother Nature pummel me again.'* I have resigned to accepting that she will have her way with me, and this is the currency of exchange for my audacious hope of seeing the elusive ghost of these hallowed halls in the Himalayas.

Our trekking resumes. Snow falls intermittently but not in a way that impedes us. It simply retouches the landscape with a fresh white glow. Monotony brings about further meditative states each day. I dive deeper, finding myself focused on my breathing, footing, and searching for six or seven hours without a single mental break or wandering. For me, this is an astounding accomplishment. Never have I meditated like this. It is my antidote to the pain the environment puts on me every minute.

I rarely consider talking at this point in the trip. Radmir and I may walk for hours with our guides, and no one speaks a word. In fact, today, I imagine we might go the entire day without any language but the language of the Himalayas: ears, eyes, nose, fingers, legs, feet, and mind all in full attention to every texture and detail. This is the antithesis of the language of city life.

 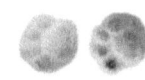

Thinking on the nature of our group's silence, I wonder about its origins. Either we all feel pressure mounting and this quiets us, or we have found comfort among each other, a safety to just be in nature, unmitigated by any distractions. I believe it is the latter. Ultimately, given the power of our daily experiences, words feel unnecessary, a distraction really.

Padma and Dorje continue each day, unfazed by the discouraging results. They rise with steeled determination, and this rubs off on us. There is wisdom in their approach.

We, likewise, have come to embrace the journey itself. Caring less and less whether or not the snow leopard can be discovered, we explore the day's meditative trance. We find it too arrogant, too ignorant, too proud to assume we should see the snow leopard. Nature tells us what we are allowed to see, and we accept it. We humbly place ourselves at her feet every day to listen, observe, and wonder at her offerings.

My mind journeys on a now-rare wander. *'I wonder what they think of us? Are they impressed with our ability to keep up with them? Do they find us acting in a way respectful of their culture, traditions, and individual selves?*

Today, like every day before it, brings fresh sores, aches, and enervation. This kind of tiredness, however, is the weariness of satisfaction. My soul, heart, and senses feel full, enriched, and enchanted by my sacred time in these heavens. I have experienced a kind of inner detox.

On the ninth day of our trip, a whole new dimension to our experience opens up to us. The community invites us to observe upcoming religious ceremonies with them. *'Let the enrichment continue. Let it surround and engulf me.'* Just when I think I have reached my limit in learning from and appreciating my hosts and their village, I am again met with greater generosity and their willingness to share their lives with us.

It is time for their New Year's celebrations. I feel a bit confused as the new year is still a few days away. Thankfully, our guides and our hosts in the homestay educate us on the differences within Ladakhi traditions and practices.

"This is Losar celebration. And our New Year." Dorje takes the time to share everything with us over breakfast. "This time is most special to us.

It brings hope and love. New things. New changes." Once he finishes sharing, Radmir and my eyes gleam with gratitude and new gleanings.

I relate this Losar festival to our current travails each day in deep corners of the Himalayan wilderness. '*I feel like a new change is welcomed in our journey. Maybe the celebration will usher in new opportunities to see the snow leopard before we have to leave this place. Or maybe I'm still too arrogant and selfish to strongarm this religious event to serve my own desires.*'

Once the many events commence, I find everything mesmerizing. It feels like Losar, Western Christmas, and wild New Year celebrations all packed into a singular cocktail of dazzling colors, flying fabrics, salivating foods, scintillating smiles, and whirling dances.

This is a feast for the senses. '*I wonder how few people will ever discover the majesty of these festivities in this terribly beautiful corner of the world. How many other "there" places like this exist that I have missed? How fortunate am I to be here now?*'

Our first experience is an observation of prayers within the home. Our host, Palden, wrapped in many thick layers of multi-colored clothes and scarves, recites Torma prayers. The entire living room beams alight, brightly, with candles, each glistening off the silver plateware. It is a bursting symphony of vibrant golden and red hues. Our faces glowingly reflect this brilliance.

Palden bends over a collection of candles and bowls of flour at a table. He takes small branches with green needles and strikes them against the bowls of flour, reciting prayers in calm intensity throughout the process. I feel lifted into another "there" I had not anticipated. The whole room swirls in prayer and twinkling candlelight reflections. This is heaven.

As I sit overwhelmed, I let myself go and just stare straight ahead. Dorje notices Radmir's and my inquisitive, but glazed-over, eyes. He leans toward us. Whispering, he explains that these prayers, "Take away bad and bring good." Dorje goes on to share that these prayers aim to ward off all bad luck, obstacles, sickness, danger, and suffering. Furthermore, they bring good fortune.

Most of the prayers and ceremonies are similar in nature as they are meant to bring peace, prosperity, happiness, and longevity. We nod silently, listening to his hushed explanations while Palden continues his prayers in the background.

Soon, these prayers consume the room, growing to a crescendo, filling the entire luminescent space. Palden breathes deeply and sucks all the evil out of the room and then exhales, throwing life and vitality back out into us and the community.

I notice dark areas in the corners of the room begin evaporating away with each of Palden's breaths. I had not noticed them before. Perhaps I had been too enraptured by our conversations to see them.

When Palden sucks in, the darkness appears again and encroaches from the corners, like a murky lung. And when he exhales, the darkness flees into the cracks and crevices.

I know this room will be rid of any darkness after these prayers, but he is not praying in our room. I am afraid my room will bring its nightly battle. The dense, dark mass will gather around my throat all night. I wish he had prayed in our room, too.

Once the festivities of the day end and we retire for the night, I am back under the blankets, and the darkness appears once again on the ceiling. Any lingering fear, however, has dissipated. *'Here we go again. Take me. I don't care. I'm in heaven, so no hellish demon can do any harm.'*

Tonight, I see proper appendages with clear form and veins and pulsating beats. Instead of descending like fog, it has a bodily form that slowly snakes down the walls and creeps along the floor toward me. For some reason, this feels worse than descending on me from above, where I can keep my eyes on it. With this new angle, where I cannot see it, fear reemerges within me.

It snarls up around me, as it swarms my throat and lungs. I struggle to breathe for a long time before I finally tire from the battle. Eventually, I fall asleep to this horror and then dream of snow leopards.

The next day repeats with the usual recon, breakfast, trekking, lunch, trekking, and return for dinner. At the end of the day, we enjoy another surprise. This time, the Losar festivities rise to a whole new level; it is not just prayers. Radmir and I sense the energy among our guides, hosts, and the villagers.

Excitement pulses through everyone. Things are stirring, and people are especially animated with laughs and enthusiasm. The pace of the village picks up as people move about more swiftly, with purpose.

"Are you ready?" Dorje asks with a beaming smile.

"Yes, absolutely," I share, humbled by the extent of blessings this community has bestowed on me. Every day is a precious gift and a fierce physical battle. Every trek on the slopes is a blessing and a death-defying step. Every new person we greet enriches us. Every pearl of wisdom from our guides lifts our spirits further, and every night, the dark mass lurks and threatens to steal it from me.

Had we not come here and experienced this "there" world of Ladakh and the Rumbak village, our lives would shine less brightly. The bank of our memories would be missing something consecrated.

What is interesting is that, had we never experienced this "there," we would never have known what we missed. *'I wonder how, in my own community where I live, I might have missed the "there" moments, taking everything I find around me for granted. I wonder how often we all do this, becoming too familiar with where we live that we miss those people and experiences who might enrich our lives.'* Ignorance can be blissful until you realize what there is to be seen, and you discover just how much in life can be missed.

After dinner, we gather outside the home. Stars glitter overhead, and the moon casts blue-tinged light across the snowcapped peaks. Like spectators in a sporting event, the peaks watch us. A fire burns brightly in the center of the courtyard, and our faces soon glow orange, just like yesterday during the prayers.

Several people take large bundles of wood about two meters in length and light them ablaze from a central fire in the courtyard. They whip the

 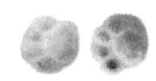

bundles around like large torches, embers dancing to the ground around them.

Loud shouting bursts of jubilation explode from everyone. People leap into action, dancing around with whirling fire torches and around the central fire. The whole courtyard explodes into a merry-go-round of fire-lit faces, shouts, smiles, blurred motions, and leaping shadows against the inner walls of the courtyard.

The reeling display stupefies me, my face painted with elation. It is a manic carousel swirling around in utter gorgeous chaos. Like a tornado, the whole movement sweeps me up with them, and I find myself circling the fire with a smile painted from ear to ear. My lungs suck in smoke, my eyes dart through the flames to see cheering faces in a blur. I am here in the hilarity of it all.

Suddenly, each person, whether child or adult, grabs a single pole or a bundle fully on fire and takes it outside the courtyard. They gather at first for a few seconds until everyone is outside, and then they dash through the maze of roads throughout the village.

Everyone shouts "Jawho" over and over, loudly, expressively. In this instant, the fiery jubilation, contained to the courtyard, now bursts into various streams of flaming light through each road of the village.

"Jawho" from this corner, the flaming pole flashing all about, embers left in the wake of the young community member.

"Jawho" from another street merging onto ours, a young man dancing and flying around the streets, a blaze of fire and embers. What begins as darkness bursts alive in light when the man arrives in the alleyway, only to see the alleyway return to darkness and smoldering embers once the young man darts away to the next road.

"Jawho" from two members behind me, passing on my left and right, dashing down the street. I step over the glowing leftover embers.

"Jawho, Jawho, Jawho" bursts from a group that has gathered at the end of a street. Up to this point, I have watched in awe as each person flies past me throughout the streets. This time, I rush to the end of the street and join this group in motion and voice. I try their chants, spinning flaming poles, and exhilarating physical displays.

I look foolish and will not pretend that any real participation is achieved. Despite this, I feel the blood pulse and rush heavily, my voice grow hoarse, and my toes bend with some warmth. I have not moved this rapidly for weeks, and this is my first time doing high cardio movement at this elevation. Surprisingly, my breath keeps up with me.

Shadows from each person in the group loom large against the nearby house walls and dance in wild, exaggerated movements. Our fires cast absurd and embellished shadows around us in a full three-hundred-and-sixty-degree turbulent storm. The whole village glows in blazing motion and fantastical, frantic, cartoonish shadows. This commotion stands in stark contrast to the silent, meditative trance I have lived in for the past nine days.

Looking to the left, I barely make out Radmir running with others on another road. We had split when I dashed to join my group. Swiftly, I sprint to him and chase with his group of people and dancing flames through the village. We step on the trail of red-hot embers left behind each person's torch. The embers light our way if we fall behind in the confusing labyrinth of roads.

I find myself laughing riotously in the whole scene. Previously, I have laughed at things here in the Himalayas, but this time feels different. I now laugh "with" instead of "at." I laugh with the community. I laugh with unadulterated joy. '*What a wondrous celebration.*' The whole experience is absurd in the best possible way.

Here I am, exhausted beyond any recent memory, feet battle-worn from the previous nine days, and still racing through tiny pathways in this remote Himalayan village in the freezing pitch-dark, chasing fire embers from waving flaming torches, screaming a word I do not even know.

What is the whole thing about? Simply, by waving threatening flames and screaming "Jawho," we chase evil spirits from the village. This is a traditional practice of supreme importance to the community.

 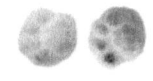

I try not to belittle it with my sincere laughter and pure joy. To them, this is a serious culmination of their prayers. I suddenly remember the darkness in our room. *'Maybe my actions have captured that thing and sent it scurrying out of this village. If I take it seriously, it might work.'*

I continue to run with them. The pace is relentless, and we cover every corner of the village. I run in this star-lit heart of the Himalayas with steel-toed boots and achy knees, all while snow leopards, no doubt, watch, perched high above.

I am sure some snow leopard watches us, elegant and erect with pride, mocking our nine days of incompetence in searching for her. *'This is the "there" moment I have fantasized about for my entire life. This is the absurdity I would have missed, had I never pushed myself to endure the cold and these daily, dangerous treks. I had to leave comfort to be in this "there" moment. This is heaven.'*

The running around culminates in a single fire at the edges of the village. We all combine our flaming poles into one pile and continue screaming "Jawho."

Then, with jubilation and satisfaction abounding, we link arms around our shoulders and walk back to our homes, satisfied that the demonic ghosts will stay away another year.

Once the commotion of the night subsides, Radmir and I retire to our room. Within minutes, we are in our beds. Darkness awaits me here and greets me by the throat again, tentacles as grotesque as ever.

I feel the varying textures of its arms: gooey, stiff, calloused, and prickly. As this is now grafted into my routine, I again welcome hell and let it have its way. Before slipping off to sleep, I wonder why my prayers and flames failed miserably to remove the demon from my room.

When the next morning arrives, the usual routine resumes. Up early, recon mission, a long morning across icy slopes, fantastic breakfast, more trekking and scoping, and a hearty dinner.

Each day for the next three days repeats, more or less, this same adventure. Some blue sheep, some traveling residents, farmers, some birds, a dead carcass or two, but no real promising sign of the snow leopard.

We find prints occasionally and one additional marking, but otherwise, nothing. The journey of these two weeks has been impossibly difficult and rewarding, if not entirely stupefying.

The silence of this trip, other than the religious festivities, has become more and more deafening, not just due to the expansive terrain but due to the absence of the ghost herself. She haunts us in her absence.

As for our room at night, the darkness continues to grow in boldness and temerity, a direct correlation with our empty attempts at the gray ghost.

The nights become more intense for me until, on the thirteenth day, I cannot continue. I have to remain in bed and rest all day while Radmir searches with the guides. I feel tackled to my bed. The disgusting beast pins me down and steals my breath. Even into the daytime now, it shows itself.

I eat and drink plenty of fluids. To rest is a luxury, though I try in vain. Palden and Dahla tend to me and help me breathe calmly and gain strength. Somehow, they walk past the dark mass without noticing it. Many hours in this day lie between conscious sickness and half-conscious, warped slumber.

By afternoon, I set myself against this evil presence and decide that it will not have me another day. I will endure the trek tomorrow, no matter the status of my health. I will win and the beast will lose. Sheer willpower shall carry me if the prayers are insufficient. This mental constitution helps fortify my physical strength, and by night's end, I know I will be stable enough and prepared for morning's rise.

Chapter 3:

Snow Leopard Walk

On day fourteen, we prepare ourselves as usual. I throw layers of blankets to the side and sit up against every desire to remain in bed. As an act of defiance, I throw a middle finger at the faint darkness in the corner of the room and rip myself onto my feet.

I feel a bit unsteady, knees weak, and ankles buckling a bit, but that fact is irrelevant. This day is our final trek, our final chance to reach into the heavens. We are set to leave the Rumbak valley tomorrow morning, and therefore, whatever pain exists will be ignored.

Radmir and I have discussed at length over dinner the past few nights about how the adventure itself has been the reward for our toils, regardless of leopard sightings. The religious and cultural events of the past few days enriched us as we felt blessed beyond the boundaries of the trip already. We resolved to accept that any hopes of seeing a snow leopard have vanished at this point. We will do a final trek on the final day to appreciate the land that has become our temporary home.

We joked that today would be the day we would see a snow leopard, but those jokes died in our soups with each sip; we had traversed every valley and ridgeline within reasonable distance to no avail. She was not to be seen. The elusive ghost of the Himalayas successfully evades yet another team of intruders.

We accept our fate with full bellies and bludgeoned feet and legs. This morning, we proceed as usual. Pack. Bathroom stop in the icy room. Scamper out with blistered feet for the morning reconnaissance session.

My arms feel bruised and weak after thirteen days of physical torment. The camera weighs heavier than ever today. My sickly weakness and the burden of my backpack and camera's weight for two weeks combine to nearly drag me to the ground. '*I may have to leave my camera behind. The*

burden of seeing feels too much to bear today.' Against better judgment, I opt to lug the camera with me one more day and endure the torment.

At this point, I barely notice the cold; it has become my companion, my initiator of meditation. The daunting push out into the unforgiving slopes once more feels nearly unbearable, but there is no other option. I will revel and glory in these peaks and sights one last time.

Radmir seems to be in good spirits. The evil spirit in our room avoided him the entire trip. Instead, I was its entrée; it feasted on me each night. The trekking itself is the only thing that makes him worn down. He seems all too eager and thankful to explore on this final day in the Himalayas.

Padma and Dorje offer us smiles and encouragement as we venture out and brave the chill. They seem to be riding the high of their celebrations over the past two days. Even still, their professionalism takes over and subdues their inner excitement. They know that we wanted to see the snow leopard, so they must make the work of today a most serious task and keep the disappointed frowns appropriately in place. *'I see past their efforts, but that's kind of them to show this level of commitment.'*

Our guides' scopes lock onto their tripods for our usual recon session. Their swiveling searches begin. I start my usual trot in the snow to keep warm, pausing every so often to hoist the camera up to my eye and help search.

After a while, I lay down on my bag and support the lens with my knees and continue searching as I have done almost every morning before. However, I am too weak today to do my usual pushups that keep me warm. I will have to accept the cold.

Radmir continues his usual routine. Pushups, slight jogging, and some stretching intertwined with searching the slopes with the Coolpix. He continues to maintain a positive attitude and a sense of gratitude for the trip.

In an instant, Padma snaps her finger, and Dorje says something in Ladakhi; the tone is terser and more forceful than usual. Their back-and-forth comments are truncated. I cannot tell what they are saying, but it is serious. They see something.

Radmir turns his head their way as well. Both he and I shuffle to them as this sudden commotion has captured our attention. Both scopes point, unmoving in the same direction. *'This is different. They haven't done this before. There's an intensity in their actions. Holy hell, is this real? Don't get your hopes up, Josh. Relax. Just find out and see what's going on.'*

As we walk up to Dorje and Padma, Radmir and I say nothing to each other. We hold our breath and plead for some interesting news from our guides.

Dorje sees it. He swings his head around with a gleam so bright his face stretches cartoon-like. His eyebrows reach so high on his head, I am afraid he is going to pull a muscle.

"**Snow leopard**!" He thrusts these words so rapidly and with a hoarse, shouting whisper. This is the loudest I have heard Dorje this entire trip, except for the Losar fire and shouts. His eyes beam, darting back and forth between Radmir and me, beckoning us to see through his scope.

'It's incredible that after all these years, these two guides have a lust for nature and the snow leopard. How many of us get bored in our jobs? The visceral elation in their bodies is wild. I want to have the same love they have for their work. I want to be in a place where an accomplishment brings out the most jubilant childlike glee.'

My thoughts do not wander far. I taste my adrenaline; it tastes like sour metal. I hear my smile; it clamors with unbridled exuberance. I feel my anticipation; it beats hard, pushing my heart to keep up with its pace. I smell my enthusiasm; one part sweat mixed with two parts stale clothes, mixed with three parts hope, and then five parts devotion.

Like a child shivering after getting out of a cold pool, I suddenly rattle and quiver uncontrollably a couple of times. Jolts of energy stream through me. I can barely contain myself.

'A snow leopard. The gray ghost. The impossibly invisible and disguised beast. The very aspirations of this trip on this final morning.' Anxiety and excitement thump heavily and hard; I can feel it through my many layers of clothes.

Padma moves to the side and invites me to look through her scope.

I run to her scope and shove my eye socket to meet its frame. *'There she is! There she is! There she is! The beautiful and impossible.'* I turn to Radmir and whisper, "Hey, I see her. Up on the second-to-last shelf of that fourth peak on that side."

"I'm on it." Dorje moves to the side as Radmir throws his face into Dorje's scope. He squeals and laughs that hearty laugh I heard on the plane. "There it is."

My knees knock, but I catch myself before falling. My sickness and the excitement have my body doing uncharacteristic things. I do not dare cry in this moment and thereby freeze my eyes shut. But I long to cry; it feels like the only bodily reaction appropriate in this absurd and wild moment.

'No, I need to see right now. I must see all this. How has a silly kid from a small, unknown town in America found his way here to this completely magical moment in the lost depths of the Himalayas? How is this real?' My hands tremor, either from the frost or the moment or both. Everything jitters inside.

Far away, about one kilometer, sits a stunning, proud snow leopard. The ghost sits erect and stares back at us. In a few minutes' time, she stands up and scours a steep, shady hillside in this young morning. *'There she is; I see her. She walks far up "there" in the heavens, beyond our grasp, beyond even a proper reach with our camera equipment. If only teleportation could be a reality. This is the first and only time in my life that I'd want it.'*

Radmir continues looking through Dorje's scope, occasionally swapping with him so that Dorje can survey the situation. If anything changes, such as her position or direction, he conveys this to us through whispers.

I hop off Padma's scope and hoist that heavy beast of a camera to my eyes. I determine, no matter my state of weakness, that I will bear this burden one last time, and I begin snapping photos in rapid-fire. Bursts from my finger holding steadfast on the shudder flow in a continuous stream. I probably rattle off four hundred photos before I pause.

In this moment where adrenaline soaks every fiber of our veins, the weight of the camera and lens becomes nothing; suddenly, these previously backbreaking tools feel like feathers. I aim, lock my back-button focus, and snap, repeating another burst of shots.

Finally, my senses come back to me, and I decide to check the LCD screen. It fails to help. I am too shaky to check things carefully, and time is too pressing with the leopard on the move to examine individual photos.

However, I do check the histogram. It is a bit underexposed, but at this time in the morning, that is acceptable. *'I can touch it up in post-processing,'* I promise myself.

Meanwhile, Padma looks through her scope and resumes tracking, feeding Dorje information with each new glance. I imagine they are trying to predict where the ghost will disappear and plan out our next scamper to gain access to another view.

Radmir now captures video through Dorje's scope on his cell phone. In pure bliss, Dorje hops up and down a few times. The happiness he gets from bringing the impossible ghost before his guests is intoxicating. I want to throw my camera down and jump with him, but I have to take more photos.

All of this euphoria occurs in near-silence. We have whispered, pumped the air with our fists, clicked several hundred photos, jumped for joy, but all of these are done in muted exuberance. Even from this distance, any sounds we make are a nails-on-chalkboard experience for the snow leopard. We respect her. So, we celebrate physically loud and auditorily vacuous. It is our silent rock concert. The spectacle of us must be a fascinating thing to observe from a bystander unaware of the context.

We sit and stir in our excitement. *'What do I even feel right now? Every emotion has collided into a nonsensical mess of something in-between, of desperation, of contentment, of happiness, of exhaustion, of hope, of wonder, of I don't know what else.*

Should I feel good? What a disgustingly inferior word in this moment. What about amazed? Am I amazed? What a terribly incompetent word. Happy? Even more inept and stupid. How to describe everything? What a waste of time to even try. No, just be in this moment. Shhh. Quiet. Be still. Just be here, "there," with her on that massive cliffside.' I still myself and continue to take photos, occasionally butting in on Padma's scope for a closer view.

I gaze and feel everything I see. Radmir busies himself with his camera, trying to capture footage. It is so far that he struggles to lock in a focus on the ghost. Dorje and Padma continue to whisper to each other and check their scopes, repeating this many times. They are concocting a plan for sure.

I stop taking photos for a few moments to try and process the moment, despite the uselessness of such a task. *'How will I describe this to others? Words only diminish and trivialize this moment. To speak of facts is to destroy this experience. You have to be here to fully understand, to have gone through our pain and struggle before this point, to have experienced nothingness, and yet everything, for weeks.*

No, a story that tells the actual truth of this experience must exaggerate in a futile attempt to approximate reality.' This realization hits me hard. There will be no proper way to share this story with others. Every attempt will fall flat if it is told as it occurred. *'How do you tell the story of meeting the supernatural with mere natural language?'*

Our guides ask for a group huddle. We all lean together, arms wrapped around each other like a team before a big game. Dorje whispers, "You know. We have big groups most of the time. We stay in valley, watching the snow leopard from far. This is the best way. The tourists stay safe and snow leopard stays safe. But, we see you both have love and respect for animals and this place, our home. We see you both strong on the mountain."

He pauses for a moment. His eyes lock with Padma for reassurance about their decision and what he will share next. "You see the snow leopard? She is very far. I think, Padma and I think, that maybe we can climb mountain and get closer. We follow behind the leopard, and see. We go slowly and carefully; we stay safe. All the time, we will show care for the leopard. What do you think?"

'Did I hear that correctly? That we can transform our here into "there" up in the heavens with the leopard? Will they permit this? Is this real? Have we really shown this much respect and gained their trust to this degree? Should I be hesitant even though my heart wants to leap immediately up there? Am I capable, in my current state, to do this?' Questions fly through my mind and plague me.

I suck in my stomach in a desperate attempt to hold myself together. The doubting questions vanish. Radmir and I both shout a whisper of "Yes" simultaneously.

We know the dangers. We understand the reverence and respect owed to every step up there. In no way will we risk harm or behavioral change on this snow leopard. This is the most sacred space and animal to us.

Thanks to our experiences and the tutelage under Padma and Dorje, we now know how to conduct ourselves in this next step. Our guides see this in us, and this instills the confidence needed for them to dare try such a thing with silly tourists. The darkness of yesterday is no more. I have the strength of a lion. *'The demons of the night have been replaced with the ghost of today.'*

Our guides nod in solidarity with our decision, and it is "game on." Dorje and Padma conduct one last check of the leopard and where she seems to be heading; she is nearly out of our view at this point.

In a scurried fashion, we pack our gear and dash off. First, we move off the plateau where we were scoping.

Next, we have to cross the river, the frozen river. As in all other crossings, the fear is not falling in, but falling on, a fall that can break any bone in your body and send you careening down the valley.

If this happens, there is no time to scamper back to this point and thereafter chase the snow leopard. Using our tripods and gravel thrown to make several paths, we safely race across the ice in record time.

For two hours, we push higher and higher. From the sting of the air, my lungs ache. We have not reached these elevations at all in these past thirteen days. My legs beg for a break, but I give them none. My hands

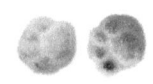

shudder in bone-breaking cold, and I slap my legs to encourage blood flow.

Somehow, something beckons me from deep down within. I forget the pain and the limitations and push on with reckless abandonment. Radmir pushes as well, just ahead of me. He is in better shape, having not succumbed to the darkness in our room these past two weeks.

Our guides are a good fifty meters further up the mountainside. They try to scout ahead to guide us by the time we get to their positions. The leopard is out of sight, but the guides think that near the ridgeline we are aiming toward, we might be able to catch a closer glimpse.

After staggering behind a bit from exhaustion, I decide to pause for a minute and catch my breath, grabbing my knees and aching for oxygen. The cliffside we climb is very long, maybe two kilometers up, so I can afford to take a break and still keep them within eyesight.

To sit and gather myself, I wander off a bit around a corner of one large rock formation. This is a rapid ascent at over five thousand meters; this practice is not for the faint of heart.

Temporarily, I rest here. Breaths heave, and my chest bulges out and then sucks in in repeated desperation for more air. My fingers shake uncontrollably now. In fact, I cannot feel my feet at all. '*Maybe I should keep moving because stopping discourages my adrenaline from taking over.*'

It is no use. The temporary courage collapses. I lay back against an orange-stained rock and sigh forcibly. '*I don't know if I can continue. This might be my limit.*'

At this moment, something catches the corner of my eye. Instead of a darting look, instinctively, I choose to gradually turn in the direction of the "something."

Snow leopard! I inhale a harsh breath of frozen air.

'*What? She is here. She is close. Very close. What now?*' My mind rushes uncontrollably with a thousand thoughts.

There she sits directly in front of me. She licks her paw and freezes, looking away from me to the west. Her closeness allows me to hear her prickly tongue licks as she grooms herself.

Other than her scraping tongue, the other sound is a faint hum from the wind, bending around the rock I rest against. I hold my breath and all movements. Her long, thick tail wraps around her body and forms a warm frame. Lowering her head, she turns and looks directly at me.

Our eyes meet and lock. She stares. No doubt, she knew I was coming for the past hour at least. Nothing surprises her in her domain. I find myself so out of breath, I have to concentrate earnestly to breathe and do so ever so slowly and with great care not to disturb her. This elevation and the sight of the ghost strips me of sanity and autonomic functions.

I pull in a breath awkwardly, forcibly, but gently. Her tail slightly curls. *'Have I startled her with that breath? Please, no. No impact on her. Let her watch me and move as she pleases. How is this real? What the hell is going on?'* As she lowers her head slowly, we both stay, in silence, in some absurd moment deep in a secret corner of the Himalayas.

Lifting her head back up, she looks deeply at me, laser-focusing her eyesight even more powerfully now. She is unfazed by my presence. Conversely, I am frozen and imprisoned by her presence. We stay here for some time, unmoving, eye-to-eye.

Time passes, and still the wind is the only thing to hear. She rolls her tongue over her nose, and her neon eyes hypnotize me. I forget what taste is. I forget the texture of the rock underneath me or the cold biting at my hands. I forget how to smell. I forget how to blink.

By lowering a bit further to the frozen ground, I make myself less threatening. Gradually, I move off the rock and sit directly on the snow. She is not bothered by this subtle change in positioning.

Again, we sit and watch each other. After some time in this odd and euphoric state, I decide to attempt a photo or video of this otherworldly situation.

Strategically and very slowly, I remove my left summit glove. Once my hand is free of the outer glove, I then settle it on my camera, hanging there against my chest. Then, I remove the second summit glove, showing great care with every measure. This hand joins the other on top of the camera.

She keeps her eyes locked onto my every minor move. Meanwhile, I keep a keen eye on her tail. It remains on the ground and still; this is important information to me, as she is neither bothered nor curious. Indifference is a positive disposition for her while we stare each other down. I want to remain unremarkable to her.

I suddenly remember my team. I wish I could scream to Radmir, but such a boisterous and unnerving act would prove asinine and extremely dangerous. In chilled silence, I hold my place and grip the camera body, fingers taut and wrapped around the textures of the hand grip and cold buttons.

In a futile attempt to maintain some blood flow and prepare my hand for an inconspicuous shot, I wiggle each finger consciously. Before I have a chance to raise the lens and take a photo, something changes.

She paws at the snow, glances down once, and then stands up on all fours. I freeze with fear. She begins moving toward me. *'No, no, please no.'*

She sways slowly, hips slightly pivoting with each step, like a slithering snake across the sand. *'What to do? I know how to handle black bears, brown bears, wolves, and mountain lions. I know how to handle African lions. But for this animal, I have no idea. There is no context for being physically near this animal other than in zoos or for medicinal and conservation purposes with a tranquilizer.'*

My mind races through scenarios, similar animals and their behaviors, and my escape plan should she come upon me. I hold my place, steady, eyes unwaveringly pointed in the direction of the oncoming ghost.

In this moment, the Eternal Knot comes to my mind once again. *'Inexplicably, here we are, interconnected, at the most opportune time and in a most deserted place. How we two beings came together in this auspicious instant confounds all reasonable logic.'*

She continues her methodical advances and closes in on me, maybe fifteen meters now. Twelve. Now, approximately ten. *'What is going on here?'* Closer. She cannot be more than five meters away now. *'She should be moving away from me, not toward me.'*

She pauses and returns her gaze directly at me. Our eyes wrestle in a contest of wills. No one budges; we peer, unflinchingly. I do not blink, even though the wind and cold burn unbearably.

If she continues further, we may be face-to-face, or even nose-to-nose. She resumes her motion, even slower this time, with more caution. She seems curious, seeking more information from this alien. However, her tail remains calm and at rest.

Her nose begins quivering and hunting for scents. She must be wondering what fool would dare tread near her home. Each new step closer takes about five seconds. Her every movement is calculated, careful, and daring.

Now she is right up on me, maybe only one meter away. If I stretch out my arm fully, I would halve the distance between us. My heart palpitations skyrocket, and my neck shivers. The knuckles on my semi-exposed hand holding the camera go stiff; I can no longer bend those fingers.

Breath slips in and out of my nostrils imperceptibly, slowly. I stiffen my neck so that even my head moves only with my shoulders and stabilizes my upper body. My right eyelid twitches under the strain.

She is so close that I can see my reflection in her radiant blue-gray eyes. I see how pathetically small I look in the glassy mirror of her reflections. The vast mountain range behind me absorbs most of the view from her eye. I am a dot. I am insignificant. *'Have I even taken a breath at all recently?'* I wonder.

Without moving a muscle, I let a tiny puff of air out of my nostrils and slyly slip back in through my slightly open mouth a single sip. Rigor mortis. I become a statue. The only option is to try and calm myself.

 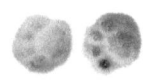

She has slowed her approach, now. The hardest part is to keep the eyes from moving. They must remain locked onto hers. No blinking, no side glances, and no wavering from the stranglehold stare.

Despite her proximity to me, I develop, in real time, a calmer sense and now see no tension or danger. Her tail stays down. Her ears still; her eyes unmoving.

Her steps slow even further, now closer to thirty seconds between each new stride. *'This is impossible.'* I begin to see everything more clearly, more in focus.

Likewise, she now senses the decreased tension in me. I am in a haunted heaven. This unearthly moment that initially elicited dread now achieves the opposite effect and chases away any fear.

Oddly, some kind of kindred bond seems to flow between this beauteous, fluffy, full, and healthy snow leopard and little, old me as we keep our eyes locked onto each other. *'No one will ever believe this. No one will ever see what I am seeing. I will be alone with the true severity of this experience. The Gods of this mountain have allowed me to take a look in ways indescribable, and that's it. To try and write about this will be a fool's errand.'*

She shuffles a few steps closer, continuing her stare. *'I don't know what I sense. Is that compassion in her eyes? Fear? Curiosity?'* I can make out individual hairs from her majestic coat of fur. They are packed in so tight and so thick. When she flexes her shoulders or legs, the hairs dance in unison and curve like foam atop an ocean wave.

Given how she is up on me now, I can reach out and touch her if I want. Of course, I would never do such a terrible thing. At this point, lost in the fantastic and exultant, I am too cold to shake. I am too shocked to run. I even forget our place here in the Himalayas.

She maneuvers once again, turning slightly until she saddles beside me and then sits down in the snow. Her tail forms a curve around her torso, and we are so close that it touches my knee. *'She. Is. Sitting. Beside. Me.'*

Complete thoughts in the form of sentences are now impossible. She has literally chosen to sit at my side, so close that we physically touch.

My mind explodes wildly into dumbstruck shock that renders my rational faculties useless. This is heaven.

I keep looking straight ahead, not bothering to turn toward her, my face still in lock with my shoulders as if I have had a neck injury. She looks in the same direction as I look, straight forward.

Here we are together on a stupid ledge, as if we should now exchange life stories. Like an old couple on a park bench, we sit side by side, looking forward, in silence.

They always say you should be in the moment. However, this moment deconstructed this ideal completely. I perceive no taste, no texture, no smell, no sound. Any hope of grounding myself in the moment through sensory experience is gone.

All that remains is sight, and even this whitewashes and narrows as if I am about to faint. What I see is too much to absorb; I am nearly blinded by my sight.

This whole insane situation of us sitting side-by-side lasts a few minutes. Another thing that people say is that these moments feel like they last forever or, conversely, that they are gone in the blink of an eye. This one just feels normal, at a usual pace, not too fast or too slow.

Suddenly, she stands back up on all fours and rubs past me, her tail rising and tickling my nose. I realize that the sense of touch has returned. I do not move a single muscle, frozen in place.

At this moment, my sense of smell returns in full force to combine with sight and touch. She smells putrid, a fully potent wild aroma. From the power of her ripe, rotten smell, I nearly gag. Within seconds, she slithers behind a rock and into a small opening in the cliff.

With haste, I stiffly rise to my feet, hoist the camera, and attempt to shoot. My right leg throbs in pain. Both feet tingle in their chilled state.

My left hand shivers and shakes the camera while my right hand is frozen stuck. I can only use it like a hammer. Any dexterity from my fingers is lost; I have to engage the shutter with the back of my knuckle. I cannot

 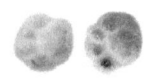

even tell where the buttons are, as I have lost all sense of feeling. '*She's getting away!*'

Finally, I will my knuckle into place and awkwardly bear the weight of the camera under my useless, frosted body, shooting rapid-fire bursts. I glance at the LCD to catch the last photo in the series. It disappoints.

The photo is taken from behind her as she nearly disappears into a valley not visible from this side of the mountain. She looks like a blurry spec on the screen. The lens will never see what I saw.

With myself left alone on this perch, the surreal dissipates, and I suddenly feel mortal again. Like a Hollywood film's gradual reveal with Dolby sound effects, my senses all crawl back to me in a swelling.

The haze of whatever I just experienced fades, and the reality of my situation comes into view. Pain attacks me, sending waves of danger signals to my pain centers.

Meanwhile, the wind, unbearably frozen air, and trickling snow tackle me and bear down hard. My dangerous footing on this ledge grips me. My eyes grow wild and large. Death is possible and near.

I remember that my team is somewhere higher up the ledge above me, likely still climbing. '*Can they see any of this? Do they know what's going on? I'm out of their sight; there's no way they saw this!*'

I gather my camera, bag, and gloves, and then make my way back to the original path where I had veered off. I look up to try to spot my team. Radmir, Dorje, and Padma have moved up very far and are now beyond my view. From their tracks, they seem to have moved to the right, off somewhere about one hundred or so meters higher.

She had escaped below and to the left, likely without them noticing. They missed all of it and will never see her again. '*I need to reach them and get help. Making my way down might be impossible in my physical state.*'

Despite my fear and pain, my mind leaps to another thought instantly. '*This is Christmas day for the Ladakhi people. I found a snow leopard on Christmas! How can you beat a Christmas like this? The bar is too high now.*' I wonder how I might ever experience a Christmas more fascinating than this one.

'*Why am I letting myself get lost in my thoughts? It's too cold up here. I'm becoming hypothermic and slightly delirious, I think. I can't feel my right hand or my feet. Why am I just sitting here thinking?*' I rip myself from the daze of pre-hypothermia and make a plan. I need to get back down. I must find a way, one step at a time.

In hopes of spotting Padma, Dorje, or Radmir, I take one last glance up across the snow field above. Nothing. '*I can't wait for them to return. I have to start closing the multi-hour gap between me and the homestay, or I'm not going to make it. Go, go, go!*'

I bear down on my teeth and grunt into the first few slippery steps in what is at least a sixty-degree vertical grade. By any standard, this is extreme "hiking." This grade on frozen snow overlooking a deadly drop-off increases the severity. Add my physical state, and this is officially an emergency.

I start my descent back down the mountain in the general direction of our homestay. My knees rattle visibly, and my stability is very concerning. Several times, at the start, I find myself slipping about a meter at a time, too weak to engage my quads and hold my position with walking lunges. Unfortunately, my eyesight begins to wane, and things narrow and become slightly blurry.

A sudden pang stings my right hand. I remember that I have been wearing only my liner gloves for this entire time. '*I'm out of it. So stupid! How did I not think to get the glove back on?*' I peel the liner glove away just a tinge to consider the damage. White blisters are forming on my wrists. Both hands feel completely numb. '*First stage frostbite! Move!*'

I wrestle the liner glove back on, along with the summit gloves. It takes far too long. I have to use my teeth, which requires pulling down my balaclava and further freezing my face.

I pull the gloves back on, but not fully. Thankfully, they are on enough to mitigate further damage to my hand. I need to descend quickly and get lukewarm water on my fingers. I lumber downward as quickly as my slumbering body can manage.

Every move sends fire messages to my brain. I am in crisis. Every downward-lunging step pounds my joints and tires me. Each step down is like skipping four steps in a typical stairwell. It jars the body, and my vision blurs even further. Due to this change in my visibility, each foot placement is filled with anxiety.

I have no idea, at this point, how many hours I have been on this mountain. It is past lunchtime for sure, and I have not had any food today. We had departed right during the pre-breakfast scouting session. Now, the rush of energy to chase it up higher has subsided, and all that remains is my body's agony screaming to me in every muscle and joint.

'If I make it, it is a beautiful kind of exhaustion. I have defied any semblance of reality and enjoyed the rarest of human experiences, and all this at over five thousand meters in some God-forsaken Himalayan ditch.'

At the end of every ridgeline I finally reach, I imagine myself closer to our original starting point than reality. I arrive at a new viewpoint and see a whole new section to navigate below.

My heart sinks with each new realization. My legs beg me to rest. Concerned, I check my right hand again; thankfully, I do not see much progression of the frostbite. I may have stabilized things, and with the level of movement, blood flow is aiding in bringing life back to my hand. My feet still cannot feel anything, though.

After what I think is about two hours of descending, I wonder, *'Did we really traverse this much of the mountain range on the way up? Did our excitement basically carry us up here?'*

My mind drifts back to the snow leopard encounter. *'How was that real? Did I hallucinate? Why did she just sit there? What was she looking at the whole time?'*

My mind races with questions and wondering. However, the deep ache in my fingers reminds me that I cannot afford to lose myself in thought again. Any thought wanderings slow me considerably.

I hear a faint scuffle above me and look back to notice that my team is returning. They are about an hour behind me, but I can make them out against the snow field.

I heave an exaggerated wave in a useless attempt to make contact. Unfortunately, all I can perceive with my current limited eyesight are their vague forms. I have no idea if they have acknowledged my wave. Assuming they will either see me or catch up to me at some point, I turn and muster my strength to trudge downward.

Every step now consists of new levels of unbearable pain and uncontrollable emotional elation. My body is a wreck. Pain receptors scream in distress while memories soar to magical heights. '*I've never been so emotionally triumphant and physically distraught at the same time. This whole day has been stupidly beautiful.*'

Like a movie, I start reliving the encounter with the gray ghost over and over to take my mind off the pain. I figure I have made it far enough down to escape death, especially with my team so close now. And so, finally, I permit my mind to drift.

The snow leopard moves toward me slowly in my mind's eye, and then, as we used to do with the old VHS tapes, the "movie" in my mind rewinds at rapid speeds, the snow leopard moving in reverse motion until back at the beginning of the capture. Repeat. Repeat. Repeat. An endless replaying of her slow, sauntering walk directly to my side.

Every new replay helps me remember, or rather see, something new: her right paw, her whiskers, the scar on her left cheek, my trembling knee, the slight stain on her tail, the perilous cold, the ray of light that poked through the clouds that spotlighted us.

After another hour and a half of trekking, I finally arrive at our initial spotting point earlier this morning. I know I have about forty-five minutes left to the homestay if I can somehow coax my body to hurry. It must be near dinner time now.

Once my feet touch the first step of the home, Palden quickly hands me water and starts a fresh fire in the living room. The numbness persists in my fingers, but my spirits improve.

Palden offers a shocked glance, likely wondering where my guides are and why I arrived in such bad shape. I nod to him and flash a smile. This is all the communication we need. Palden knows what I have seen. A moment of silence and knowing smiles hold us together for a few seconds.

Then, he leaves me briefly and returns shortly after with tea. I swallow butter tea and devour leftover bread. As we are off the typical schedule, Palden was not ready for us at this time. Despite this, he graciously scrambles to help, aware of my distress.

I breathe deeply and slowly. With time, the trauma will subside, my warmth will return, and my hand will heal.

Minutes later, Padma, Dorje, and Radmir arrive. They see my face, and it reveals the story.

"Don't tell me you...," inquires Radmir. I force a smile on my still-frozen face, ice particles still clinging to my beard hairs.

"What happened?" asks Padma.

"We lost you for a while," notes Dorje. Then he notices my labored breathing and trembling hands. "How can we help you? Are you okay?"

"No way in hell. You saw her, didn't you? Radmir can't leave his question until it is answered fully. Each of the three encircle me and look on without blinking. I pause. Then I muster some strength. Then I pause again, too tired to speak. Then, finally, I let it out.

"I saw her. She saw me," I softly reply, under the weight of my heavy breathing.

They crowd around the fire for an early dinner and tales of insanity. This time, I had the tale to tell. I knew what it was to be "there."

~~~

As I get into bed for the night, I settle under the blankets and realize something: the darkness and its tentacles are gone. *'What happened? Where did it go?'*

I wonder if some leftover residue from today's ghostly encounter has scared away the demons of our room. Finally, the darkness has left us. I can see more clearly in tonight's "night" than on any other day on this trip.

The next morning, I move stiffly. The extra climb from yesterday has added significant and debilitating sores and pains on top of everything I had already put my body through these two weeks. Both hands feel numb at the fingertips. The white blisters on my wrists from the day before are now more pronounced and show clear signs of early frostbite.

Despite the physical pain, my emotional and mental states could not be more satisfied. The sheer delight of this trip will stay with me forever. Every few final moments mix gratitude with discomfort on this final morning in the Rumbak Valley.

Gradually, we pack every bag and head downstairs. Palden and Dahla beam with smiles and wish us good luck on our journey home through physical gestures and Ladakhi phrases we do not understand.

But we do understand, even if the details of the words are unknown to us. We see them and understand their hearts after receiving their hospitality and love for two weeks. For them, if we see, then the whole village sees. We are together and we are because of each other, similar to the central idea of the Ubuntu Spirit.

This is an unlikely partnership, with people from several wildly different backgrounds and contexts. Beauty personified. Without our hosts, guides, and entire village, we would be lost.

I glance one more time at my Eternal Knot tattoo. '*We are bound together by this experience. Forever, we are connected to this breathtaking village and beautiful people.*'

I reach over and hug Palden. He squeezes me tight and pats my back. Then, I turn to Dahla. I bow, humbly, and hold her right hand in both of mine. While I cannot feel her hands due to my frostbite, I know that I have communicated my gratitude. An overwhelming, tear-filled emotion passes over me like a wave.

 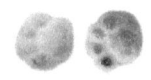

Radmir turns and repeats the same gestures. Finally, we turn to the outside courtyard as Padma and Dorje meet us there.

Once again, we burden the donkeys and strap everything to their backs. Every painful step on our blistered feet and every inhale of icy air are now coupled with the extra layer of indescribable gratitude. How can we possibly articulate our appreciation for such an experience?

You can see pride and relief in the interactions of Padma and Dorje. The pressure had been mounting with every unsuccessful day. We were not the source of this pressure; their desire to please and pursue excellence was the source.

Those joking tones and lighthearted dispositions we noticed at the beginning of the trip once again return to both of them. '*What a delightful mix. They imparted wisdom day after day. They showed us the way. Yet, they don't take themselves too seriously. They know how to balance being serious and having a good time.*'

They laugh and chatter back and forth in Ladakhi for the entire three-hour journey back to the van waiting just outside of Leh. '*I imagine they are arranging for a party this evening with good local liquor. More importantly, I'm sure they're thinking about reuniting with their families and their respective villages after this arduous journey.*'

In contrast, Radmir and I return to the silence of previous days. Our minds are lost in recollection. The memories from the previous two weeks plays on repeat. Every cliff edge, every ceremony, every lunch at 5,000 meters, every evening scamper back to the homestay for a scrumptious and steaming dinner, every false alarm, and, of course, the final sighting itself. The blur of everything now comes into focus in my mind's eye.

With each memory I replay, a smile forms under my balaclava. My left hand aches; my heart warms from the ecstasy of adventure. This is the mantra of the trip in its physical form: terribly beautiful.

At last, we reach the van. This time, we choose to ride in silent reflection. Dorje and Padma now fully observe the satisfied silence that rests on Radmir and me, and they match our energy out of respect.

For the final night of the trip in Leh, Radmir and I laugh and reflect over dinner. Padma and Dorje join us for this final supper.

"It feels like we've experienced a lifetime with you both in just two weeks. Thank you," I say to Dorje and Padma, who sit across from us.

"You are welcome. We are honored you come to our home and see everything," responds Padma in her usual cheery voice.

"Yes, we are grateful you have come and experienced our life," adds Dorje. "We hope you understand a little about us and our customs. And we hope you enjoy seeing the snow leopard. I know, for you, Josh, this was extra special being so close to the leopard."

I nod, still overwhelmed by the whole thing. "I need more time to process it all." I chuckle with inexplicable gratitude.

"Thank you both," Radmir adds with deep sincerity in his voice. His voice did, in fact, come to represent the trip. The depth of our experience is now felt by both of us, and his deep tones match this feeling.

"Please come back again," suggests Padma.

"I will, I will," I promise.

As I board the flight home, I think about my promise. Even though I should avoid trying to distill the entire experience into writing, I will try.

I decide to write a book. *This will be my act of returning. I will return again and again and again through the narrative. I will revisit this adventure by painting an image of the experience, and every time I pick up the book, I will step up into the Himalayas and breathe the cold air.*

I look out the window and take one last glance at Leh as we launch into the sky. This time, the entire city and the surrounding slopes can be seen crystal clear. There are no smudges on the window.

I lay back and slouch, softly into the seat, and dream. I dream she's there with me on the plane in the next seat over. She licks her paws and turns to stare at me with her laser blue-gray eyes.

 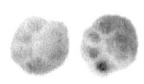

Themes

This book, and the entire series, explores a range of themes and concepts. One primary exploration found in this story is how *we often possess a distorted view of beauty and conflict*. Rudyard Kipling once wrote in his poem "If":

> "If you can meet with Triumph and Disaster
> And treat those two impostors just the same;"

While I agree that both, personified as they are, can be imposters, I am more interested in a slightly modified version of this. I find that in triumph, there is disaster, and in disaster, there is triumph. It is not that they are fake, but they blend and are actually the same in so many situations in life.

Therefore, I wish to examine the interconnectedness of the terrible and the beautiful. Much of life is both difficult and beautiful, and I feel this is worth exploring and accepting. Dangerous things are often beautiful. Beautiful things are often dangerous.

For example, Mother Nature is personified in this text to exemplify the complex relationship we have with her; she is the giver and taker of life. Likewise, we both protect her and destroy her.

To understand life thoroughly, we need to see how our oft-polarizing beliefs and perspectives fail to truly "see" reality. There is beauty in your struggle and struggle in your beauty. The sooner we recognize and examine these areas in life, the better.

To properly see beauty and conflict is to accept the nuance and complexities within these human experiences.

Closely related to this theme is the *difficulty of truly seeing what we encounter in life*. We "see" people, but do we really see them? We "see" our pain, but do we really see it? We "see" ourselves, but do we fully see?

 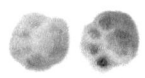

The act and the result of seeing is a terrifying thing—to realize you have looked and still fail to understand, or see, what you just observed.

What is more, is it even possible to see anything fully? Maybe this is a fool's errand. Should it not be the case that seeing ourselves is the easiest of all possible tasks? And yet, do you truly understand your own self, or are you regularly surprised by your own actions, behaviors, attitudes, and thoughts?

How might we humbly realize that we must become students of ourselves and the world, actively learning and growing in our act of "seeing" and understanding? How might we humbly admit that we cannot fully see anything?

If we cannot make such an admission, then we are doomed to deceive ourselves, imagining we have fully seen. This is how stereotypes quickly form, and we make "others" out of everyone who does not "see" things our way.

As such, seeing becomes life's great burden. If we struggle to see. And if we struggle to even realize this about ourselves, then this is our burden.

To truly see is to embark on a life-long journey, an adventure really, that seeks to see and understand. Either we walk in ignorant darkness, or we walk in burdensome awareness. Honestly, most of us inhabit the space in between these dichotomies.

Additionally, *it might be beneficial to see things partially*. Sometimes we are not meant to see fully. At times, it is best to see only part of what we wish to see.

Knowing or "seeing" something completely can cause harm, distrust, frustration, anger, and so much more. In fact, there are times when we force things and ruin our actual view.

Like the plane window I unintentionally smudge at the introduction, our futile attempts to see might hamper our ability to see the truth, rest in the moment. Wisdom is knowing when acceptance of "knowing in part" or "seeing in a mirror dimly" is necessary and advisable.

Furthermore, **we should be careful what we choose to see**. There is a warning to be tactical in what you aim toward. Things are not always as they seem. If you look and set your sight on it, you will find it. This can be invigorating and empowering. It can, likewise, be destructive. We must be cautious about our aims and look with intention. Not all things in life should be gazed upon.

In summation, to "see" is the single most challenging human enterprise. Many wars and abuses on large and domestic scales have been levied due to the lack of seeing the other. We must learn to see. We must seek to understand. It should be our life's work.

While not a fully articulated theme, a thematic topic that emerges is **the desire to explore "there."** The old adage that the grass is not greener on the other side can be true. However, it can be used as a weapon to beat down our ambitions and chain us to our own yard.

So, while the cautionary tale suggests that things are not always as they seem, things may also be greater than they seem. We must allow for this possibility.

Human beings have an innate yearning to explore and find adventure. This does not mean we have to travel to experience these. No, exploration and adventure can be found in our "backyards." It is in front of us and requires a mindset to seek it out, even in the mundane, everyday routines. As I mention in this book, *"Whatever lens you choose colors the world you see."*

Therefore, the grass on the other side is a "there" worth exploring. You can always return to your "home," but life is too fragile, too fleeting, to spend it boxed into a small life, with a small mind, and small experiences.

Another thematic topic is **humanity's destructive and restorative interaction with nature**. I am interested in our disturbances and the preservation of nature. We both build up and destroy. We cause harm, and we attempt to give back.

In fact, to order to live, to see, to explore, some degradation of nature occurs. Wherever you are reading this book, the ground below you was

once undisturbed, undiscovered, raw land. Even now, your very act of living squashes the natural state below you.

We need not feel shame in this. This is the great paradox—to live is to destroy. We do what we can to mitigate damage, and we live onward.

Another area of exploration is **the profound impact of women in Ladakhi society**. While humans can be destructive, it is the Ladakhi women who have played an instrumental role in the restoration of the snow leopard and the simultaneous support of their villages.

From their ideas, to their brute strength; from their arts and crafts, to their hospitality; from their conservation efforts, to their monetary contributions; so much of the success story of Ladakh is dependent upon the intelligence and power of women.

As such, I intentionally changed the sex of one of my guides to reflect this. I highlight the work they are doing, from artistic efforts in the homestay to bearing the weight of stacks of wood in the blistering cold.

Furthermore, Mother Nature is feminized and shown as both beautiful and dangerously strong, an apt metaphor for the women of Ladakh. Even the snow leopard is honored as a female.

Another thematic topic is **the confusing sense of defining utopia (heaven)**. Maybe heaven will never live up to its reputation. Maybe heaven has a bit of hell in it. Maybe hell has a bit of heaven in it. How we define our heavens, how we think about them, and how we go about trying to find them are particularly interesting.

At this point, it should be clear that the themes from this series seek to expose false dichotomies and stereotyped polarizations. Almost all that we encounter in modernity pushes people into echo chambers that oppose the "other."

People, ideologies, places, events, and groups are deemed wholly evil or praised naively. We have lost the art of nuance. We have lost the conversation. We have lost our sight. We sit in our corners of the sandbox and throw at each other, petulantly, like immature children.

We have built strawmen, false caricatured representations, of the "others" in our lives. There is no utopia. There is only the space between heaven and hell, and we all, as humans, embody the full range of these. Let us extend grace to each other and revive our curiosity in each other.

It is time we rediscover the art of nuance, and the art of re-engaging with the "others" in your life. We must commence meaningful discussions and learn to "see" each other more thoroughly.

This leads to a final thematic topic: *the elusive search for authenticity*. On this adventure in life, what is your tale's tale? Is it one that finds the truth of the thing, or is it one where you feel boxed in and stuck? Or maybe it is a tale about looking at things without ever seeing them.

What ghost do you chase? And how will you see it? What lengths are you willing to go to in order to find that elusive ghost of authenticity?

May this fictional, but true, memoir inspire you to find your own adventure, wherever you are, and may that adventure be in the purpose-filled quest for authenticity and truth.

Join in the Journey

Dear Reader,

Thank you for joining me in my journey into the Himalayas among the people of the Rumbak Valley. This is the first book of a multi-volume series of fictionalized memoirs of my travels and adventures. If you enjoyed this book, then read each of the travel books in the series.

Also, you can see the real travel experiences from this book and from the other books on my YouTube, Facebook, and Instagram spaces:

http://www.youtube.com/travelingteachr

https://www.facebook.com/travelingteachr

https://instagram.com/traveling.teachr

For the trip explored in this book in particular, search for "snow leopard" on my YouTube channel to find several videos, including an insightful interview with a leading snow leopard conservationist.

Most importantly, if you enjoyed this book, I ask for a review from you. What you share will help readers discover these stories and pass them on to others.

You can leave a review, detailed or brief, on Amazon, Audible, or Goodreads.

Sincerely,

Joshua Smalley

134

Book Series Introduction:

A Confession

I have a confession: I'm crazy. I believe life must be lived on the razor's edge of safety and danger. For me, the hallmark of a satisfying life is pushing limits, challenging perceptions, and daring to defy fears. Seeking adventure in the extreme adds color and texture to life that would otherwise be undiscovered in a more sedentary and comfortable lifestyle.

This way of living is not for everyone; this is why I can comfortably adopt the label of "crazy." It is contrary to the norm and sometimes contrary to our biology.

Going on an "adventure" has become a more popular endeavor as more people rise out of the extreme poverty of past ages and find more time and money to explore. Furthermore, the rise of influencers glamorizing "adventure" and travel has made such options true bucket list pursuits.

For me, however, not just any adventure will satisfy. No, it must be quirky, unique, and obscure. If the common tourist trap adventure company lists bungee jumping, I usually run in the opposite direction, seeking something more off-the-beaten path and more authentically and viscerally human.

The possibility to see, learn, or enjoy something very different from my previous lived experiences calls me out of my bedroom, into the wild, and into the wilderness. This, again, makes me atypical and a little crazy.

Sometimes I break from this ideal. Occasionally, my idea of a vacation is a well-trodden path worn flat by tourists' shoes. My trips may include a comfortable hotel on a nice beach or a walk on cobblestone walkways in well-worn corners of Europe.

Even while I indulge in such trips, that inner call to nature and adventure whispers to me. It mocks my reclining chair, massages at noon, tour in the evening, toes in sand, and drink-in-hand lounging.

While not for everyone, my natural bent draws me toward thrilling adventures and a quest to meet people and places often overlooked.

 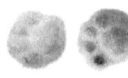

How do I "adventure"? This is my process: pick a location, Google-search or AI-search the craziest things to do in that location, and consider all nature or wildlife options not already on the 'craziest things' list.

This gets the ball rolling. Some ideas start to take form. Then I dig deeper. What genuinely crazy adventures avoid the clichéd and hyped pseudo-adventure trips typical of those wet-behind-the-ears, Instagram-show-and-tell travelers?

Joking aside, we love them; that is why they are famous influencers. Most love the gems they discover and promote. Without them, we would not know about those lavish, vacation-worthy places to explore around the world.

For me, however, I have to return to what is natural. Digging deeper considers the most unusual people, places, events, and adventures I can find. How can I go about encountering something truly different and do so responsibly?

I filter the list by the wildest options available. I consider any ethical concerns or limitations. Then I contact some people who live near the intended destination to gather more accurate intel.

At this point, I begin to edit and revise the list as necessary. Reflection is a good strategy at this point as I consider mistakes made in past travels and adjust accordingly. Finally, I proceed with full commitment and a dash of reasonable caution.

While I pursue this, the irony is not lost on me. This whole system serves as a sort of self-deception. When I, a regular run-of-the-mill, Walmart world, small-town American, pretend that I can embark on authenticity in unfamiliar environments, I must admit that it is a fool's errand.

I seek out adventure that attempts to escape the whole tourism space, but I am, and will always be, a tourist. Sometimes I feel that even my hometown is foreign, and I play the role of tourist.

These short-term adventures cannot plug me into a new place and groups of people in any true sense. It is a façade. I cannot access authenticity in these experiences and adventures. I am an outsider, pretending.

I may observe. I may attempt to participate. I may share my story as if I were "there," but the truth is that an outsider like me with my privilege and ignorance cannot fully appreciate, understand, or empathize with each new encounter.

I will forever be a mere visitor, allowed to enter the hallowed spaces of others. I feel blessed to see and understand something unique through my experiences.

Why adventure then? The reason is that the partial taste of beauty I discover about the world in this type of travel is worth the risk and price of admission. While not fully genuine, it is still something that has the potential to radically change the way I know myself and see the world. And so, I adventure onward.

I share my stories to share myself and the enduring truths I have learned. The details of my stories are true and untrue. Enduring truth resides underneath the details, be it fact or fiction, and lives with me always.

I am forever indebted and grateful to everyone I have encountered on these journeys. Thank you for your generosity, patience, kindness, helpfulness, constructive criticism, and love. I am nothing without all of you.

My story is your story. My truths come from you.

References

"Butter Tea." *Wikipedia*, The Wikimedia Foundation, 2025, en.wikipedia.org/wiki/Butter_tea.

"Double-slit Experiment." *Wikipedia*, Wikimedia Foundation, 17 July 2025, en.wikipedia.org/wiki/Double-slit_experiment.

"Dragontail Peak." *Washington Trails Association*, www.wta.org/go-hiking/hikes/dragontail-peak. Accessed 24 Jan. 2025.

"Gothic Basin." *Washington Trails Association*, www.wta.org/go-hiking/hikes/gothic-basin. Accessed 24 Jan. 2025.

"Handicraft Development." *Snow Leopard Conservancy, India*, Snow Leopard Conservancy India Trust, www.snowleopardindia.org/handicraft-development.php. Accessed 22 Jan. 2025.

"Interview With Snow Leopard Conservation Director, Dr. Tsewang Namgail | Himalaya Snow Leopard Trip." *Traveling Teachr*, 4 Feb. 2020, www.youtube.com/watch?v=WC5xd0Emeck.

Kipling, Rudyard. "If—." *Poetry Foundation*, 1943, www.poetryfoundation.org/poems/46473/if---.

Matthiessen, Peter. *The Snow Leopard.* 1978, ci.nii.ac.jp/ncid/BA18380266.

"Mount Shuksan." *Washington Trails Association*, www.wta.org/go-hiking/hikes/mt-shuksan. Accessed 24 Jan. 2025.

"New Year Celebrations in Ladakh." *Peaceful Societies*, University of North Carolina at Greensboro, 1 Jan. 2009, peacefulsocieties.uncg.edu/2009/01/01/new-year-celebrations-in-ladakh/. Accessed 22 Jan. 2025.

Nietupski, Paul Kocot. "Tormas: Ritual Offerings Connecting Humans and Deities." *Project Himalayan Art*, Rubin Museum of Art, 2023, rubinmuseum.org/projecthimalayanart/essays/tormas/.

Accessed 22 Jan. 2025.

Project, Tibetan Nuns. "Eternal Knot Symbol." *Tibetan Nuns Project*, 28 Apr. 2023, tnp.org/eternal-knot-symbol.

"Rumbak village." *Rural Tourism*, Ministry of Tourism, Government of India, 2023, https://www.rural.tourism.gov.in/Rumbak-wildlife.html.

Sahapedia. "Petroglyphs of Ladakh." *Sahapedia*, 2024, www.sahapedia.org/petroglyphs-ladakh. Accessed 3 Sept. 2025.

Sartre, Jean-Paul. *No Exit.* Archive.org, 1994. www.ia600303.us.archive.org/13/items/NoExit/NoExit.pdf. Accessed 28 Feb. 2025.

Sidorovich, Vadim. "Where and What Is Naliboki Forest?" *Naliboki Forest*, 1 Nov. 2018, www.nalibokiforest.info/post/where-and-what-is-naliboki-forest. Accessed 28 Feb. 2025.

Sidorovich, Vadim. *Zoology by Vadim Sidorovich.* sidorovich.blog, 2024. Accessed 28 Feb. 2025.

"Sound, Visual, & Display Technology." *Dolby*, Dolby Laboratories, Inc., 2025, www.dolby.com/.

Thakur, Shikha. "100 Tibetan And Sherpa Names For Baby Girls And Boys." *MomJunction*, 17 Feb. 2025, www.momjunction.com/articles/tibetan-sherpa-names-girls-boys-meanings_00680269/. Accessed 8 July 2025.

Thasngspa, Tashi Ldawa. "Petroglyphs of Ladakh." *Sahapedia*, 2024, www.sahapedia.org/petroglyphs-ladakh. Accessed 28 Feb. 2025.

The Holy Bible. Bible Hub, 2025, biblehub.com/1_corinthians/13-9.htm.

The Holy Bible, English Standard Version. Bible Gateway, www.biblegateway.com/passage/?search=1%20Corinthians%2013%3A12&version=ESV.

"The Truman Show." *IMDb*, IMDb.com, 1998, www.imdb.com/title/tt0120382/.

"Three Fingers." *Washington Trails Association*, www.wta.org/go-hiking/hikes/three-fingers. Accessed 24 Jan. 2025.

"Tower of Babel." *Britannica*, www.britannica.com/topic/Tower-of-Babel.

"Wild Edible Plants of Ladakh." *Himkatha*, www.himkatha.org/wild-edible-plants-of-ladakh. Accessed 8 July 2025.

www.ingramcontent.com/pod-product-compliance
Lightning Source LLC
Chambersburg PA
CBHW050414110726
47899CB00008B/2709